PACIFIC BOOK REVIEW STAR

Awarded to Books of Excellent Merit

Author Sheila Munds-Belbin takes readers back in time to World War II in this historical romance and thriller.

Allison[1] is an interpreter and her unique language skills also enable her to be a spy since she can speak both English and German fluently.

She has several close calls while spying and with the Gestapo that adds to the readers' suspense and will have the reader biting their nails.

---

[1] The author originally used the name "Allison" for the character. However, she had it changed to "Alice" to honour the memory of her grandmother.

In Beloved Enemy, Munds-Belbin has created
a character that is irresistibly engaging.
Her tortured yearnings in love and with duty
causes the reader to alternately rejoice,
cringe, and scream with frustration.

Readers will not be disappointed with Beloved Enemy
and there's a bit of something to offer every kind of reader.
Those looking for a good romance will find a sweet love story;
those wanting suspense won't be
disappointed in the espionage;
and, those looking for historical accuracies will be delighted
with this feminist version of international espionage.
In the end,Alice's weaknesses as a character are revealed
to be very human weaknesses and readers will struggle
with each decision that she makes
while debating how they would handle such moments—
as a heroine true to her convictions or as
a woman torn between two loves.

-PACIFIC BOOK REVIEW

RECOMMENDED

by The US Review of Books

Set 70 years in the past, Alice Grant takes on one of the most dangerous missions a woman could engage in during World War II. As a member of the British military, she agrees to go deep undercover within Nazi Germany, going straight to the heart of the turmoil in Berlin.

Well-written and relatively quick moving, the story focuses on the inner challenges of the character faced with such deep-seated internal conflict. Loyalty to country wars with her dedication to love and an internal desire to be happy. Having made her choice, the book follows through in a non-linear fashion, exploring the consequences of such a choice, and bringing in additional characters to peripherally explore other potential responses.

- THE U.S. REVIEW OF BOOKS

Belbin's debut novel delivers a stirring World
War II tale of forbidden love—
and its tragic fallout.

English spy Alice Grant finds a once-in-a-lifetime love
with a German officer in this wartime novel.
Posing as a beautiful German interpreter
named Hildegard Hessler,
she goes on a mission to seduce Colonel Karl Von Richter,
an attractive intelligence operative.
Overall, Belbin offers a powerful and memorable tale.
This story of treachery in the name of patriotism
is gripping and suspenseful,
as much a love story as a tale of self-discovery
and laden with history and psychology.
Alice's return trip to Germany proves just
as courageous as her first one,
and she emerges as a heroic figure—
a truly captivating, complicated heroine
whose choices may haunt readers
long after they reach the last page.

A highly original WWII story of one woman's
inner conflict and ultimate triumph.

- KIRKUS REVIEWS

A tale of love and loss during wartime,
Beloved Enemy is a romantic thriller
that features one young woman
who risks everything to spy on the
Germans during World War II.

Alice is an intriguing character in Beloved Enemy.
She is strong, yet also vulnerable as she
becomes conflicted about her mission.
Readers will quickly become engrossed in the story
and emotionally invested in Alice,
as they hope she'll find a happy ending
and come to terms with her past,
despite the horrors she must face.
The secondary characters are also interesting;
the author does a solid job examining the
effects of war on ordinary people.

The narrative writing in Beloved Enemy
is sure-handed and polished...

...the story is engaging and entertaining.
Fans of romantic thrillers will enjoy immersing themselves
in this complex and well-written novel.

- BLUEINK REVIEW

A bilingual woman in the British Women's Army
sneaks into Germany during World War
II to seduce Karl von Richter,
a Nazi intelligence colonel,
and ultimately falls in love with her enemy.

In a gripping story that spans twenty
years, beginning in 1942,
this courageous heroine sacrifices her safety and well-being to carry out her assignment. The book follows her psychological adjustment and relationships thereafter.

The situation may be offensive, painful,
and difficult to comprehend,
yet Belbin succeeds in writing high-impact,
conflict-ridden historical fiction
that will appeal to connoisseurs of war stories.

The prose is filled with period detail,
enhancing the sense of place in war-torn Europe.

...Belbin knows how to capture a reader's
interest from the first page and not let go.
This ability is not mastered easily, and she
flaunts the skills of a seasoned professional
in creating page-turning drama.

- FOREWORD REVIEWS

SYNOPSIS

This powerful tale has been critically-acclaimed by book experts. Inspired by a true story, the book covers a twenty-year period beginning in 1942. It follows the life of a spy from the British Women's Army who was sent to enemy-occupied France during World War II to seduce a German Colonel who worked in intelligence and who is involved in troop movements.

A highly original story, the novel explores the effects of war on people's lives while keeping its central focus on a mission that helped to determine it's outcome.

This is a little known story of bravery and heroism… of risks and sacrifices… and the conflict between dedication to love and loyalty to country.

ISBN-978-1-9163-4640-6 (*sc*)
ISBN-978-1-9163-4641-3 (*eb*)

BELOVED ENEMY

INSPIRED BY A TRUE STORY

*The greatest dilemma
is when love
conflicts with duty*

SHEILA MUNDS—BELBIN

Contents

Chapter 1

CHANCE MEETING

The meeting at staff headquarters had ended sooner than anticipated, but Major Andrew Sinclair couldn't face returning to his base. He was thinking about Alice and how much he'd missed her during the last few weeks when he suddenly spotted a familiar figure walking towards him. "Janet, I can't believe it," he said as she came close.

"What are you doing in Oxford?"

Janet stopped dead in her tracks. "Good heavens, it's you, Andrew! What a surprise," she said, smiling. "I've just finished doing a job at a house outside town, so I'm staying here tonight. I'm taking the opportunity to do some shopping for myself for a change." Then she added, sounding like an afterthought, "Jon is away at a medical seminar and won't be home until late tomorrow."

"Well, look, I'm staying here too, so why don't we have dinner together and swap news?"

He was pleased when Janet agreed, for his mind was in turmoil. He welcomed the opportunity to talk to someone. It would be better than turning the same thoughts over and over without reaching any conclusions, which was what he had been doing.

It was not until she returned to her hotel that Janet realised how exhausting the shopping trip had been. She lay on the bed to rest before getting ready for dinner with Andrew. She thought about what a coincidence it was running into him, for she had been thinking about him and wondering how he was feeling about Alice's sudden decision to go to Germany. She had always liked Andrew. At one time, she used to wish that he would show some interest in her, but that was before she met Jon. Anyway, he'd been in love with Alice ever since he'd met up with her again at an army reunion not long after the war ended. That was more than nine years ago. Now Alice had gone off to Germany on what seemed to be an unplanned visit, without saying how long she would be away.

Alice was her best friend, yet her behaviour was often puzzling. The two women met while serving in the British Women's Army during the war. Alice had married a young flying officer named Philip Grant. Only six months after they were married, his plane was shot down, and he was reported "Missing, presumed dead". Janet did her best to comfort Alice. That was how they became close friends.

As she lay there reminiscing, she was reminded of those dark days during the war when they all just lived for the present, never knowing what the next week, or even the next day, might bring. One day Alice had announced that she was being sent away on a special assignment. The next day she was gone. No one seemed to know where she'd been sent or for what reason. It was two years before she returned, and when she did, she found that Philip Grant was alive and in a prison camp in Germany.

After the war, neither of them wanted to continue with the marriage. They'd grown too far apart and eventually divorced. It was amicable, however.

Janet used to worry about Alice because she was never able to settle down to life as it used to be. Of course, many people had difficulty settling back into civilian life at first, but most managed to pick up the threads at some point. It was not so with Alice, though. The lively young woman that she had once been no longer existed. Janet often wished that Alice could find the right man and marry again, but she never had. Many men had shown an interest in her, but none of them mattered to Alice until a year or so ago, when her long but casual friendship with Andrew seemed to blossom. Suddenly, they were always in each other's company. People began to think of them as a couple. Janet knew that Andrew had asked Alice to marry him, and she'd tried to find out from her why she refused. Alice simply said that she didn't want to remarry yet. *Perhaps things are coming to a head between them,* Janet thought. She lay there on the bed for some time, thinking about various friends from the war years and wondering what they had made of their lives.

When she noticed that daylight was beginning to fade, Janet got up to unpack some of her shopping bags. She selected a blue dress that she had bought that afternoon. Taking it over to the long mirror in her room, she held it up in front of her and, smiling at her reflection, decided that she would definitely wear it for dinner that evening.

Janet Lane was a striking-looking woman with short fair hair and a good figure. She was the sort of woman who was envied by other women because she managed to look elegant no matter what she wore. This dress particularly suited her and was perfect for an early summer's evening. She felt like dressing up. She had to admit that she was looking forward to having dinner with Andrew and to one more night without the kids, much as she loved them.

Having changed into civilian clothes, Andrew sat in the bar of Janet's hotel, waiting for her to arrive. Although he was ten years older than Alice or Janet, he was still a good-looking man. Before the war, he'd married and had a son. When his wife left him for a wealthy banker, she took the boy with her.

Glancing up now from his paper, he spotted Janet as she was entering the bar and jumped up to greet her. "I know that you like French food. There's a little French restaurant where Alice and I have dinner sometimes—I thought we might eat there," he suggested.

"I'd like that very much Andy," she said. The restaurant was typically French. Monet and Cézanne prints hung on the walls, and there were red-and-white check tablecloths on the tables.

"Alice likes to eat here," he said. "It reminds her of her student days in Paris."

After they had ordered the meal and the waiter poured the wine, he sat looking at Janet. He wondered why he hadn't realised before what a beautiful woman she was. His obsession with Alice must have made him blind, he thought.

He smiled at her. "You look nice."

"Thank you," she said, smiling back at him a little self-consciously. She was pleased and wished her husband would sometimes pay her a compliment. Jon always seemed to be preoccupied with other things these days.

"You know that Alice has gone to Germany," he said. Janet nodded. It was obvious that Alice was constantly on his mind. "Actually, she phoned me from there a week or so ago and said she would be staying a while longer. She also said that she would be going to the South of France before she returned home. I don't understand it. It's all so mysterious. Why has she abruptly gone off to Germany on her own?"

Andrew had been staring into his glass. He looked up. "Well, she tells me she has to confront her past... and that she must do it alone. I think she really does want to come to terms with it; she has never been able to face going back there before. If she faces up to her past, maybe she can then make some decisions about her future."

Janet knew what he was referring to. "We are always expecting to hear that the two of you are getting married," she said.

Andrew shrugged his shoulders. "Perhaps she has told you that I have asked her several times but always get the same answer: 'Maybe one day, but not now.'" He sighed and shook his head. "But I'm patient because I fear I may be largely responsible for her problems. I know that I must take some of the blame at least."

The waiter arrived with the main course, which he placed before them, and this lightened the mood.

"It looks delicious," said Janet.

He grinned. "Well, it's much better than I would have had if I'd gone back to the base tonight!"

During the meal, they chatted inconsequentially.

When they finished, Andrew lit a cigarette and a few moments later stubbed it out. "You know, of course, that I was in intelligence during the war," he said.

Janet nodded. "Yes, I know that."

"Well, it was part of my job to select suitable men and women for missions abroad; most were sent into occupied France to work with the French Resistance, but one or two went into Germany as spies. They were carefully chosen... and Alice was one of them. It was I who selected her."

"But I always thought she went to France," she said, surprised. "Why did you select Alice to be a spy? Was it because she spoke German?"

"Well, no, there was rather more to it than that."

"You know," said Janet, "in all these years, she's never told me much about the time she was away, except that she was sent behind enemy lines. She came back a very different person from the Alice I knew before. I assumed it was because she had matured, as we all had. I simply concluded that whatever she did had to remain top secret.

But all that was a long time ago."

Andrew nodded in agreement. "Yes, a long time ago, but not for Alice. I don't think she has ever been able to forget about those years she spent in Germany. I led the debriefing when she came back. I believe she told us only what was absolutely necessary for us to know. There is no doubt that she did the job she was sent to do, but I am certain that a hell of a lot happened that we know nothing about. She refused all offers of counselling at the time, you know, and as you say, she has never talked about any of it since." He sighed, "I used to think that she would tell me more eventually, but she never did, and whenever I have tried to raise it, she has outright refused to talk about it. I just gave up in the end. This decision to go back there is a new development, and in a way, I welcome it."

"Poor Alice," said Janet. "I had no idea. It accounts for so much. There must be something terrible that she has had to block out... that she hasn't even dared to think about."

"Yes, something like that, I suppose," he said. "I just hope that when she returns, she'll feel more able to get on with the rest of her life, preferably with me, but if not with me, then at least with some other chap." Taking off his glasses, he rubbed his eyes. He looked tired. "I'm retiring from the army soon," he said, "and I want us to make a new life together. I don't want to lose her."

"I know, my dear," Janet said sympathetically, "but you must try to be optimistic about the future. I know Alice loves you."

"I am not even sure that she does anymore," he said sadly. Then, reaching across the table for the wine, he poured them both another glass.

"Now," he said, changing the subject, "suppose you tell me what's been happening to you and Jon since we last met. It must be nearly three months since we came to see you for the weekend."

"Yes, I suppose so," agreed Janet.

They talked about her latest job, redesigning the interior of the country house near Oxford, and Jon's new job at the laboratory in Reading. Then she found herself telling him about some of her own problems. She hadn't intended to burden him, but things just came out.

"Jon started having one of his bouts of depression a month or two ago. I've begun to wonder if we can continue to live together anymore. I expect we'll sort it out because we have to for the sake of the kids."

Janet had been a widow when she'd met Jon. Like Alice, she had married during the war. Her husband was killed at the time of the Normandy landings, soon after Alice's return. When the war was over, she met Jon, a young doctor. They married and had two children, Matthew, now age six, and Peter, age four.

When Andrew saw tears welling in her eyes, he placed his hand over hers. "Want to tell me about it?" he asked.

Janet wiped away the tears. "You have enough worries of your own."

"Look, you and Jon are my friends, so please tell me what's wrong. Maybe I can help," he said gently.

Ever since Andrew had known him, Jon had suffered from spells of depression. It was something those who knew him just accepted. Fortunately, he'd seemed able to control them quite well in the past.

"Jon won't talk to me about his problems anymore," Janet said. "We're growing apart. There's nothing I can do about it, Andrew, except wait and hope that he'll go back to being as he used to be—when we were happy together. He hardly notices the children these days. I think one of my worst moments was when Matthew asked me a few weeks ago why Daddy doesn't love him anymore. Again, Jon seemed to get worse starting a month or two ago. I know that he often felt frustrated in his work at the hospital, and I think it has to do with his experiences both during the war and since. He has had to treat the wounded. He has seen so many young men disfigured for life, yet he can do little to help."

Her face brightened. "There is one good thing. Since he has been doing research work at the laboratory, he does seems to be a bit better, so I'm telling myself that things will improve one day."

Andrew tried to comfort her. "Knowing you both, I'm sure you will sort it out. I think you're right—if he is more content now, the situation between you will improve. Perhaps he's more suited to research than to hospital work, you know."

She nodded and attempted a smile. "I think perhaps I should be getting back now, Andy," she said. "I must make an early start tomorrow because I have to collect the kids. They've been staying with Jon's mother."

She insisted that she could take a taxi back to her hotel alone, but Andrew wouldn't hear of it. The night had turned chilly when they left the restaurant, and they were pleased that a taxi came along right away. When they arrived at Janet's hotel, he suggested they have a final drink. They went into the small bar, ordered their drinks, and sat down. Both of them felt they had somehow been drawn together by their difficulties.

"It helps to share one's problems, doesn't it?" he said. "I'm really glad we met up."

"So am I," she agreed.

"To future happiness for both of us." Andrew raised his glass.

"And to Jon and Alice," said Janet.

After a few minutes, he stood up. "I guess I'd better let you get that early night," he said. Then, as he was leaving, Andrew suddenly took her in his arms and kissed her on the lips. He knew at once that he should not have done it.

He apologised immediately.

"Don't worry, I'm not offended. And I promise not to tell Jon!" she added, laughing.

He still felt embarrassed as he said goodbye. It had been his intention to reassure her, not to make a pass at her.

Although it was chilly, he decided to walk back to his hotel because he needed to think. The cool night air might sharpen his mind. He was certainly missing Alice. They didn't live together, but he stayed at her apartment whenever he could get away. He wished he knew what to do. Perhaps he should have tried harder to persuade her to tell him more about her years in Germany. But had he insisted, he knew it would only have upset her. He had always feared what he might find out. That was the reason he was worried now about the outcome of her visit.

He kept wondering what memories had been aroused in her. What sort of man was von Richter, the man on whom he had sent her to spy? How well did she get to know him? How did he treat her? Was he a cruel man? These questions had haunted him for years. He felt that he could no longer keep waiting for answers. He decided that when Alice returned, he would tell her that if their relationship were to continue, they would have to face the past together. They couldn't go on as they were. He had to know the whole story, whatever the consequences.

As his steps quickened, Andrew's thoughts turned to Janet and her problems. He wondered why he could not have fallen in love with someone like her. She was considerate and loyal. She knew what she wanted from life. He remembered the way she used to look at him years ago and guessed that she had been interested in him then. *Jon must be a bloody fool,* he thought. He had always considered him a self-centred sort of chap. Now, if he wasn't careful, he might lose his wife altogether. However, he could understand Jon's frustration as a doctor, being unable to help people maimed and scarred for life because of war. *Jon's a casualty of war himself,* he thought.

Sadly, Jon and Alice had deep scars, ones that did not show. They both seemed unaware of the feelings of those who loved them. He could not remember Alice shedding a tear in all the years he'd known her. *She seems to lack something,* he thought, but he could not fathom what it was. He wished she had the softness and warmth of Janet.

Still, it was a fact that Alice fascinated him. Perhaps it was because she had lived amongst the enemy, something he doubted he could have done himself. Her toughness combined with her delicate blond beauty made her an enigma. It was a pity that despite all their years of friendship, there was still a barrier between them. He knew that he had to break down that barrier somehow.

Chapter 2

MIXED NATIONALITY

When Alice Grant's plane landed, there was no one at the airport to meet her because she had not said when she would be returning. After being away for nearly a month, she felt that she needed time alone before seeing any of her friends, especially Andrew. Luckily, she was able to persuade a taxi driver to take her the one-and-a-half-hour drive home.

As she pushed open the front door of her apartment, she saw a heap of mail lying on the floor. She gathered it up and placed it on her desk without opening any of it. She decided to attend to it all another day. Flopping down on the sofa, she realised how tired she was. She felt drained. But it wasn't due to the length of the journey. Such a lot had happened in the last few weeks, and she had shut out so much over the years. It was as though she had been numb for all that time. Then feeling abruptly returned. All the tears she had never been able to shed now flowed; at last, she had faced the past and been able to mourn.

Wearily she got up, poured herself a drink, and placed it on the small table beside her. Looking round the room now, she was glad to be back. She had always enjoyed her home. Located just outside Oxford, it was part of an old mansion that had been converted into separate apartments. Alice's was on the ground floor, looking out onto lawns, terraces, and distant fields where cattle grazed. Sometimes it reminded her of another garden in a place where she had once been so happy.

For a small apartment, it was furnished luxuriously, with soft velvets, brocades, and deep pile carpets. A little antique desk and chair, where she sat to do her work, stood at one end of the sitting room. There were bookshelves along the entire opposite wall. Some of the shelves housed well-chosen ornaments, but mostly they were packed with books, some old and rare, which she had inherited from her father. Apart from a few items of jewellery, her father had directed that all his personal effects were to be sold. The books, however, he had left to her specifically, expressing a wish that she should retain them.

As a freelance interpreter and translator, she didn't have to go to an office every day. She took assignments through her agent and worked from home, translating books and documents. She was fluent in several languages, so the work paid quite well. Best of all, she could give herself time off when she needed it. Indeed, she had allowed herself a month or so for the trip to Germany, so she had plenty of time now to think about the happenings of the last few weeks.

Alice was a petite woman with fine features, blue eyes, and blond hair which fell in soft waves to her shoulders. There was a look of vulnerability about her appearance, which had at times proved a considerable asset. Men seemed to want to protect her, and she was able to take advantage of this.

She lay awake that night thinking about her future plans and thought about inviting Janet to stay with her for a few days. Janet often visited, and they would go on shopping trips together, but it would be for a different reason that she would be inviting her to stay this time. Alice felt that at last she wanted to tell someone about the years she'd spent in Germany during the war. She no longer needed or wanted to keep it all to herself. Janet was the one person she thought might understand.

Janet arrived two days later. Putting her suitcase down in the small hall, she hugged her friend.

"Oh, Alice," she said. "While you were away, Andrew told me where they sent you during the war. I had no idea—why did you never tell me about it? I am so sorry. You must have suffered so much without telling anyone."

Alice gave her a smile. "Settle yourself down," she said, "and while you're unpacking, I'll get you something to eat." Having ignored Janet's remarks, she moved towards the door but then stopped. "It's not what you think, you know." She disappeared into the kitchen.

Janet took her case to her room, and by the time she returned, Alice had made coffee and sandwiches. They sat down together, two old friends who had over the years shared their sorrows and problems as well as the good times.

Alice hesitated. "I don't want you to be sorry for me," she said.

Janet looked puzzled. "What do you mean?"

"I don't want you to think that I was tortured or physically harmed in any way—quite the contrary, really.

All I ask is that you don't judge me too harshly. My own sense of guilt is my punishment."

"I'm here to listen, not to judge you, you know that," said Janet. "You're my best friend, and I care about you. I just want to help."

"I know." Alice paused to adjust some cushions behind her. "I don't want you to be hurt by anything I am going to say," she said. "You see, there are things you don't know about me, things I didn't want to tell you before. Believe me, Janet, it's not because I didn't trust you. No one knows my whole story, but now I want you to know everything. Please don't tell anyone else, though, not even Jon and especially not Andrew. I shall have to tell him eventually, I know that, but not yet... and anyway, there are things I cannot tell him because I don't want to hurt him."

"All right," Janet said, "you know I'll say nothing if that's what you want."

Alice took her time. "It may come as a surprise to you to know that I am half German," she said. "Father was English, but my mother was German. I spent many years in Germany with my parents when I was a child, so I came to know parts of Germany well."

Janet was staring at her in disbelief as Alice continued. "As you know, my father was a diplomat. Before the war, he worked at the British Embassy in Berlin. Whilst out there, he married a young German woman, my mother.

They came to England just before I was born. When I was five years old, father was sent back to Germany in a more senior capacity, and of course, Mother and I went with him. We lived at the embassy, and I was brought up and educated out there until I was eleven years old. By that time, I was bilingual. I suppose that's what started my interest in languages and made me want to become an interpreter."

She looked at Janet, who was listening intently, and then continued. "Most of my young friends were German. There were one or two English youngsters living at the embassy, children of other senior officials, but I didn't regard any of them as my special friends because I had started to think of myself as German like my mother. To me, Father was the foreigner."

By now, Janet was recovering from her initial shock. "It's hard to take it all in," she said. "I have always known that you speak several languages, but I find it difficult to think of you as German."

"That's because I'm English," Alice replied. "Remember that I was born here in England and my father was English."

"I know, but it's just something I didn't expect. I suppose the war has not been over long enough for me to have forgotten how we felt about the Germans."

"Dear Janet, what I am saying must come as a shock to you. I understand that but bear with me. I remember when Father was recalled to England; I didn't want to leave Germany and hated it back here at first. But I soon readapted to the English way of life and made new friends. Then, about two years after our return, and I think much to my parents' surprise, my mother became pregnant. It was a difficult pregnancy. She died in childbirth, and the baby died too. It took me a long time to get over the death of my mother. Father was heartbroken, and after a while, he sent me away to a boarding school and returned to Germany to take up another post at the embassy. He came back from time to time to visit me, but mostly I spent holidays with my school friends and their parents. I suppose it was inevitable that Father and I would grow apart."

"You'll have to forgive me, Alice," Janet interjected, "but I must ask you why, in all these years, you never told me any of this. Not even that your mother was German... You must have known that it wouldn't have mattered to me and wouldn't have affected our friendship." "I know," Alice said, "but during the war, how could I have admitted to my friends that I'm half German? Then, later, I was told not to mention it to anyone or to talk about my mission abroad. Anyway, it was something I wanted to forget."

"Did Andrew know your background?"

"Yes. He chose me for the assignment because of it. Do you remember that day when I had compassionate leave so that I could go to Winchester to see my father, who was by then terminally ill?"

"I remember that you left in a hurry," Janet said.

"Well, it wasn't that my father's health had suddenly deteriorated further; it was because it was likely that if I agreed to do the job that Andrew wanted me to do, I would never see my father again. You see, my assignment was to be of indefinite duration and likely to last beyond his lifetime. In any event, I might never have returned.

Andrew had met with me the day before and told me what they wanted me to do but said that I didn't have to agree to it. I was told to think it over and was sworn to secrecy.

"When I saw my father, I didn't tell him much. I just said that I might not be able to visit him again for a while if I accepted an assignment abroad. I think he may have guessed that I had been selected to become a spy because he reacted by saying that I must do whatever my conscience told me was right. My father was a patriot in every way and, although he didn't actually say so, it was obvious to me that he thought I should do what was asked of me. When we said goodbye, I think we both knew that it was for the last time. Although Andrew had told me that I didn't have to agree to the mission, apart from what my father thought about it, I knew that it was expected of me."

"How dreadful to put you in that position," Janet said. "You must have been so frightened. I know I would have been terrified."

"Yes, I was, but I realised that I was an obvious choice. After all, I was a widow, or so it was presumed, with no relatives apart from an ailing father. In addition, I was fluent in several languages, which could be useful." Alice smiled. "Well that's about it. Perhaps it will help you to understand when I tell you about some of the things that happened. I don't know how much Andrew has told you about his role in British intelligence."

"Not much," said Janet, "except that while you were away, I ran into him in Oxford. We had dinner together. He told me then that he was the one who sent you to Germany to become a spy. I couldn't believe that he had sent you there."

"Well, as I said, he did tell me that I didn't have to accept the assignment. It was made absolutely clear to me that if I was caught, I was unlikely to be treated in accordance with the Geneva Convention. As a spy, the best I could expect was to be shot. I knew the risk I was taking. I made my decision the day after seeing my father. You may remember that the next day I told you that I might be transferred to take on another job quite soon but that I wasn't at liberty to tell you anything else."

"Yes, I remember well," said Janet. We had an impromptu party for you that same night, didn't we?"

"Yes, that's right. After that, my whole life changed. Nothing was ever the same again. The next day I was sent away for a six-week course. During that time, I was trained to parachute from a plane and among other things how to use a gun—a handgun, that is—and how to fit a silencer. They even told me to start thinking in German so that I wouldn't be taken by surprise at any time and reply in English. When I got into Germany, they said I had to be guarded about what I said and try not to show my feelings too much. It may help me to survive.

With those words ringing in my ears, I was declared ready to go and given my suicide tablets and a last-minute briefing."

Although Alice had known Janet for the better part of ten years, she realised that Janet must be finding it difficult to accept all the things she had been telling her. Janet had once said that after Alice returned, the tale was told that she had been in occupied France and Janet had imagined that she had lived as a French girl, perhaps even fallen in love with a member of the French Resistance, because that would explain her attitude to other men when she came back home.

Alice, sensing some of what Janet might be thinking, smiled at her. "I'm still the same person, you know," she said. With that, she got up, went over to the small drinks cabinet on the other side of the room, and replenished their drinks before sitting down again.

"I've told you all this to help you understand why I behaved the way I did. Ever since I returned, I have been trying to forget the two years I spent in Germany. I refused to remember because it was too painful. I can tell you that I lived the equivalent of a lifetime in those two years."

"You know," Janet counselled, "Andrew loves you, but I think he's becoming impatient. He won't wait for you forever. And perhaps you needed to relive some of your past to be able to accept it and get on with your life."

Chapter 3

ENTRY BY PARACHUTE

It was a cold night in the spring of 1942 when Alice Grant sat shivering in the plane as she prepared to parachute into Northern France. Making the jump into enemy-occupied territory, and not knowing what she would find when she landed, it was very different from the organised jumps she had made during training. This was the real thing, and she struggled to conceal her fear. She heard someone shout that it was time to go, and as she stood poised and ready to jump, someone else called, "Good luck." Then she was out.

It was a successful landing. She had been told that members of the French Resistance would meet her. A man would identify himself as Antoine, speaking to her in English. She was to reply in French that her name was Nicole. Just as she had begun to collect her parachute together in the way she had been taught, she saw two men running towards her. One was a large burly man, and the other was smaller. Her heart was beating wildly. *What if they're not members of the Resistance?* she thought. She was not sure what she would do in that event.

The small man approached. "I am Antoine," he announced.

"Je suis Nicole," she said with a smile. "I'm thankful to see you."

He spoke now in French. "Hurry—follow me. Don't worry about the parachute. My friend will take care of it."

He ran towards a wooded area, and she followed closely behind. When they reached the woods, he put down a bag he had been carrying on his shoulder and spoke quietly.

"Take off your jacket and jumper and put on these clothes," he said, unzipping the bag. She did as he ordered. "What's the matter with the clothes I was wearing?" she asked.

"Nothing, but these are better. They're French," he said. "The trousers you have on—are there labels inside them?"

"No. I removed them."

"Good. People have been caught out before by the clothes they were wearing, especially by the labels inside them. Now put this over your head," he said, handing her a black scarf. He stuffed the clothes she had discarded into the bag. By now, the big man had arrived. He snatched up the bag.

"It has gone as we hoped," he said. "Au revoir et bonne chance." With that, he was gone.

Antoine was a man of indeterminate years, and she thought that perhaps he was a farm worker.

"We have to travel on foot for about twelve kilometres, so we must not waste time. I would like to get away from here as soon as possible." She nodded in agreement. "I am taking you to a safe house," he said.

For the next hour or so, they tramped in silence, mainly through wooded areas, until they came to a clearing, where he indicated they could take a brief rest.

"We are making for a farmhouse which lies just beyond a small village," he said as he offered her a drink from a bottle which he had pulled from his pocket. "You must stay there for a while, until we know that it will be safe for you to leave."

"Will you be taking me to the border?" she enquired. "No," he said. "My job will be done when I deliver you to Anna, who owns the farm. Someone else will escort you on the rest of your journey to the German border. Now, if for any reason we are stopped when we reach the village, I shall say that I am taking you to see my sister. You say as little as possible."

"I understand," she said.

"We should move on now." He seemed anxious. "We still have a long way to go, but we can rest again later."

He led the way across fields and along country roads. By the time he said they could rest again, she was exhausted.

"We must time it so that we arrive at the village about an hour after curfew is lifted," he said as they sat down on the ground.

He produced the bottle from his coat again. They both drank. It contained red wine, which she didn't much like but drank gratefully nonetheless.

"Soldiers have been billeted in the village, so we must be extra careful when we are there."

By now, it was starting to get light, and Antoine wanted to move on again. It was about two hours later when they reached the village and saw two German soldiers approaching. Antoine grabbed her arm and pushed her into a doorway.

"Don't forget what I told you. When they are near, we will turn out of the doorway as though we have been visiting someone. Try to look as though you are unconcerned by their presence."

She did as she was told, and as the soldiers passed, Antoine nodded and wished them good day. They responded cheerfully, and Alice breathed a sigh of relief when they passed out of sight.

"Your next guide will probably have identity papers for you to produce when required during the rest of your time in France," he told her.

As they walked on through the village, people were pulling up blinds on shop windows, opening shutters, and laying out their goods. Food was rationed and in short supply, but there were vegetables and fruit on display. Fortunately, no one took much notice of the two strangers, and they left the village without further incident.

Alice was growing ever wearier as they covered the final part of the journey and was thankful when Antoine pointed out the farmhouse in the distance. When at last they reached their destination, she was taken to the rear of an old whitewashed building and into a courtyard. A woman came out from the house to greet them and ushered them into a typical farmhouse kitchen. Vegetable soup was cooking on a stove, and nothing had ever smelled so good to Alice; the aroma filled the air.

The woman smiled, addressed her as Nicole, and introduced herself as Anna. She greeted Antoine enthusiastically and beckoned them both to be seated at the table, where she placed bread and cheese before them, followed by bowls of the hot soup. Then she turned to Alice.

"First you eat," she said, "and then we can talk."

They gratefully ate and drank wine. When they finished the meal, Antoine announced that he would rest for an hour or so and then be on his way. Before he went, he wished them good luck. Alice thanked him warmly for meeting her and escorting her safely to the farm. Finally Anna and Alice were left alone together.

"You will be staying here for two weeks, maybe longer," Anna said. "Tomorrow Marcel will come, and you will meet him. He will be your guide and will tell you when it will be safe for you to leave."

"Will he be staying here?" Alice enquired.

"No, he owns the neighbouring farm but comes here every day and brings produce from his farm. In exchange, I give him food that I have prepared. It works well for us."

Anna was a woman whose face made her appear older than her years, but it was a kindly face. Alice liked her immediately and felt she could trust her.

Anna then told her about a German officer who came to the farmhouse occasionally but seldom stayed for long. "I give him a glass of wine as well as food to take away—and perhaps some fruit and vegetables or bread which I've baked. If he thinks we are sympathetic to the Germans, as some French people are, then he is less likely to suspect us of being involved with the Resistance. It means, though, that it may be necessary for you to keep out of his way. Marcel will decide what you should do.

Now, you are tired from your journey, and you should rest. I will take you to your room. I hope you will find it comfortable."

Alice followed her up some steep stairs to a surprisingly pleasant little room, although the washing facilities were a bit primitive and consisted of a jug of cold water which had been placed in a basin on a washstand. The bed, however, was soft and comfortable when she lay on it. She was tired and thankful to have come this far safely, and she soon fell asleep.

The next morning, she awoke early to the sound of a cock crowing and realised she must have slept for the rest of the previous day. It was only five o'clock in the morning, but country life started early, so she washed and dressed and went down the stairs to greet Anna.

Anna had been collecting newly laid eggs and placing them in racks. "You're up early," she said. "We can have breakfast together."

Breakfast consisted of bread rolls with jam or cheese, all made by Anna, followed by a jug of hot milk—or coffee when it was available. After they had eaten, Alice asked if she should stay in her room. Anna thought it would be best for her to keep out of sight until Marcel arrived.

"Do you think the German soldier will come today?" "He may," replied Anna, "but he never comes before midday, and Marcel will be here before then."

"Why do you do this, Anna?" Alice asked. "It must be dangerous for you having people like me staying here.

You're putting your own life at risk. You don't have to do it, do you?"

Anna smiled. "Oh, but I do. You see, my husband was a soldier, and I have not heard from him since France was occupied. Wherever he is, I know that if he is alive, he will be fighting for France. Members of the Resistance bring people here to me, and by allowing them to stay, I too am fighting for France. I do not know the real names of any of you, where you come from, or where you are going, and it is best that way. The less information I have, the less I could tell the Germans if they questioned me."

Alice nodded. "You are so brave."

"No more than many other French women and you, my dear. How about you? How old are you?"

"Twenty-three," said Alice.

"So young. How I hate this war. I wish you luck, child, in whatever it is you are doing."

"Thank you, Anna," said Alice, "and thank you for all your kindness. I shall wait in my room now until Marcel arrives."

It was not long before Anna came to tell her that Marcel was there and waiting to see her. They went down the stairs together, and Anna took her to a room on the other side of the house. As soon as they entered, Marcel came over, shook Alice's hand firmly, kissed her on both cheeks, and told her that he would be her guide for the rest of her time in France. Anna excused herself tactfully, saying that she had work do.

Marcel indicated a chair where she could sit at a table.

"I have managed to obtain some identity papers for you," he said. "They should be sufficient if we're stopped en route but perhaps not good enough to use at the German border. Your German guide will sort that out. It's usually my job to bring people out of Germany; this is the first time I have been asked to help someone get in there." He grinned broadly.

He seemed a confident young man, probably in his late twenties. *He must have been a soldier before joining the French Resistance,* she thought.

"What about the German officer who comes here?" Alice enquired.

"I would advise you to avoid him when possible, but if he sees you, don't worry. I shall probably be around when he comes and will introduce you as my cousin. We'll tell him that you are taking a short holiday and staying with Anna to help on the farm. I don't think he will ask to see your papers, and if he does, I doubt that he will query them. He likes too much the food and wine that Anna provides. Anyway, even if the Germans know someone parachuted into the area recently, they are more likely to be looking for a man—and certainly not a young woman such as yourself. In any case, I have been told that you are being sent on a special mission, and that we must take every care to ensure that you are handed over safely to our German contact."

Alice could tell that he thought her unsuitable, and he was surely thinking that they would be looking for someone who was not only older but more experienced. "I'm sure that you will do your best for me, Marcel," she said with a smile.

Every day she made a point of keeping to her room between the hours of eleven and two. It was three days before the German came, and she successfully avoided him, but his next visit was different. He came much earlier in the day than usual. Alice was sitting at the kitchen table, peeling and chopping vegetables. Luckily, Anna was there too when the door opened suddenly and in walked the German.

Anna greeted him. "You are earlier than usual, Captain, but not too early to have a glass of wine, I hope," she said, bringing a bottle and glass to the table. "This is Marcel's cousin, Nicole—she is staying with me for a few days."

Alice had to remind herself mentally that her name was now Nicole.

Marcel had been within earshot and entered the room. "Good day, Captain," he said. "I was about to leave, but I think I'll have a glass of wine with you before I go."

Anna put bread and cheese on the table for the two men.

"You have met my cousin?" asked Marcel.

"Yes," said the German, eyeing her. "Where are you from, Fräulein?"

"From Paris," she said. "I live on the outskirts, so I am enjoying a visit here in the country."

Paris was the one city she knew well, having studied for a year at the Sorbonne, so she was ready for any questions he might ask.

Marcel interrupted the conversation. "I have yet to take my cousin on a tour around the area." Turning to Anna, he asked, "Would you mind very much if I take Nicole with me today?"

She indicated her approval, and the captain looked disappointed. "I hope to see you another time, Fräulein,"

he said. It was easy to observe that he was looking at her appreciatively rather than with suspicion.

Yes," Alice said, "but I am only here for a short time.

Please excuse me now, Captain, as I must get ready to go with Marcel."

"Until next time, then, Fräulein," the German said, standing up and giving her a formal bow.

After he left, Marcel turned to her. "We must consider what is best to do next. You speak our language perfectly, whereas the captain does not, so I am sure he has no reason to be suspicious. I think his interest in you is for a different reason. We should perhaps let him see you once more so that he will not think that we are concerned about his presence while you are here. Then I think we should move on as soon as possible."

Alice nodded her agreement.

"Is your German as good as your French?" Marcel enquired.

"Better," she said. "Don't forget that I expect to be meeting many German soldiers before long." Somehow she felt he was not too confident about her ability to be an agent. She hoped she was wrong.

"I think you should come with me, and we will not return to Anna's farmhouse for a while. We can go to my own farm, and I will saddle up some horses. You do ride, don't you?"

"No, I don't," she replied.

"Well, now is your chance to learn!" he said, laughing.

Then he put his hand on her shoulder. "We should not always be too serious, Nicole. If I appear light-hearted, it is because, doing the work that we do, I would not survive if I were not that way. Today I shall be having a day out with a pretty girl, so I am happy, but—do not worry—I shall not make advances towards you. That is a pleasure I cannot afford!"

"Something tells me that you are a very nice man, Marcel."

"Yes. Unfortunately I am," he said with a smile.

Marcel's farm was much larger than the one that Anna owned, and he had told her that he ran it with the aid of several farmhands. Before going off to saddle up the horses, he said quietly, "Remember that you are my cousin and that some French people are collaborators."

She stood waiting for him to bring the horses out, hoping that the one she was to ride would be small and docile. Marcel then helped her mount the one he had chosen for her and walked the horse round for a while until she became used to it; then he mounted his own horse and led the way to the fields at the side of the farmhouse, where they took a gentle stroll.

Alice enjoyed the experience much more than she thought she would, but when they returned to the stable yard and Marcel helped her dismount, she cried out, "Oh my God—I don't think I shall ever walk again!"

Marcel was really laughing at her now. "Don't worry," he said, "you'll feel better soon. You need to have a warm bath. Come into the house and we'll make you comfortable."

They went inside, and he showed her where the bathroom was.

"Would you like me to rub your back?" he joked. "No, I would not," she said loudly.

"Pity," he said, laughing again.

He was right; she felt much better once she bathed.

Later she and Marcel sat together enjoying boiled eggs and a bowl of Anna's vegetable soup.

After an hour or so, he said he should take her back.

She would have liked to ask him about his life before the war, but people in their circumstances did not ask questions about each other's private lives. Instead, she thanked him for rescuing her from the attentions of the German and making her day so pleasant. Then he took her back in his old van and explained the situation to Anna.

After he'd left, Anna came and sat beside her. "He is a good man," she said. "He has risked his life many times to help others."

"What I have seen since I came here has moved me very much," said Alice. "Antoine and his compatriots, you and

Marcel... and I'm sure that there are many others like you, all risking their lives in the fight against the German occupation. I hope that one day we shall all meet again to celebrate victory."

"Yes, so do I. Some of us will survive, but I am afraid that some of us may not. Please God, victory will come before too long," said Anna.

Alice wanted to get into Germany as soon as possible. Although she dreaded the thought of it, she was at the same time impatient to start the job that she had been sent to do. She liked Anna and was always pleased to see Marcel, but even so, time dragged.

The German captain came again, and as arranged, Marcel left her and Anna alone with him. Alice played her part and chatted to him easily in her fluent French. She made a point of asking him about his family and where he'd lived before the war. He was clearly pleased to tell her.

Anna provided the usual glass of wine, together with a bag of freshly baked rolls for the captain to take with him, but they were both pleased when he said that he could not stay for long on that occasion.

As soon as the captain had gone, Marcel entered the room, and it was agreed that he and Alice would leave the following day, travelling in the old van.

The time quickly came for her to say goodbye to Anna and for them to set off on their journey to the German border. Marcel told her that they were going to a café on the outskirts of a small town, about half a kilometre short of the border, and that the German agent would be there. When they arrived at the town, Marcel stopped the van on a side road near the café.

"You must do exactly as I say," he said. "We will go in there together and order something to drink, and then about ten minutes later, I shall say goodbye and leave you, but first I will have pointed out to you your contact, who will be sitting in the café. He will be your guide from then on and will take you into Germany. He is a very experienced agent so don't worry. The arrangement is that a few minutes after I have left, you too will leave. You will turn left out of the café and walk slowly to the end of the road. By that time, he will have caught up with you and will stop you and ask if you know the way to the station. You will reply that you are going that way yourself."

"Yes, I understand," she said. "Now we must go," said Marcel.

She put her hand on his arm. "You have done so much for me, Marcel. I hope that we shall meet again."

"I hope that I shall be bringing you out of Germany when we next meet," he said as he embraced her. "I wish you luck, Nicole. Be careful and may God go with you."

She felt sad saying goodbye to Marcel. She would miss him; she had felt safe with him.

They went to the café and acted out the charade as he had explained. Her guide was there, sitting in a corner and reading a paper. She waited a few minutes after Marcel had gone before leaving and slowly walking to the end of the road as instructed. She could hear footsteps behind her, and soon the man had caught up with her. When they had exchanged words, he introduced himself as Otto.

"There's a bookshop around the corner," he said. "We will go in there."

As soon as they entered the shop, they were quickly ushered into a back room.

"We have to be discreet, Fräulein," said Otto, "because it is best that you are not associated with me too much. Although I shall be one of your contacts while you are in Germany, your main contacts will be Herr Franz Hucke and his wife, Lotta. You will be staying with them."

He did not smile or shake hands as Marcel had done. Instead, he pulled some papers from the inside pocket of his jacket.

"These are your identity papers," he said, spreading the documents out on the table. "You will take the identity of a young woman of the same age as yourself. She died in Africa and has no living relatives. Her death has not been registered over here. Born in Germany of a Swiss mother and a German father, her name was Hildegard Hessler, and from now on, that is to be your name. We can add a photograph of you later, but the one attached will pass for now. You could perhaps put up your hair to look a little more like her, for the purpose of crossing the border," he suggested. "You must get used to speaking only in German. Most people living near the border are bilingual."

"Yes, I will do that," said Alice.

She had noted everything he had said. Now she had to forget that she was Alice Grant and become Hildegard Hessler. For just how long, she had no idea.

The realisation of what she was doing had finally caught up with her. Although she was pleased to be starting her assignment, she was at the same time afraid of what the future might hold.

Chapter 4

A NEW IDENTITY

Otto had arranged with Lotta that she would be on the station platform when they arrived at their destination in Germany. Although he had travelled in the same compartment as Hildegard, he had been at pains not to let it appear that they were together. He told her to walk close behind him when they got off the train in order for Lotta to pick her out from the other passengers who had alighted at the same time. As the train pulled up, Hildegard spotted a tall well-built woman standing at the end of the platform, and as she came near, the woman ran up to her.

"How lovely to see you, Hildegard," she said in a loud voice, kissing her on both cheeks. It was obviously a show for onlookers. "Come," she said. "I have a car."

They hurried along the platform and were watched as she handed in her ticket. Lotta indicated a small car parked just outside the station, and when they were seated in the car, Lotta turned to face her.

"Well, with your blond hair and blue eyes, you certainly look German. You are a natural blonde, of course?"

"Yes, I am," Hildegard replied.

"Good—that is important," said Lotta. She gave her a brief smile before continuing. "You must be pleased to be here at last. Your journey has taken longer than expected."

"I am anxious to start the job that I was sent here to do."

Hildegard was becoming irritated by the charades in which she had been involved, although she understood the need for caution. Lotta was right; the journey had been a long one—too long. It had made her impatient.

"Herr Hucke will explain what is to happen, but first we must get to know each other. You will need time to get used to our ways and the conditions under which we live here."

Lotta seemed pleased when they arrived in time for Hildegard to be introduced to her husband before he left for a meeting. After he had gone, she picked up Hildegard's small suitcase and took her to her room.

"We propose to explain your presence here by saying that I was a friend of your mother, who died some years ago, that I have known you since you were a child, and that you regard me as your aunt."

"Do I call you Lotta or Aunt?" Hildegard enquired.

"Either will do," she said. "Now, Fräulein, come back when you are ready. I will prepare refreshment for you. I believe tea is the drink you English prefer."

Hildegard began to feel more at ease. They spent the rest of the day together and Lotta told her something about life in Germany but said nothing about the assignment; she was obviously waiting for Herr Hucke to talk to her first.

As she had expected, the next morning Herr Hucke suggested that she accompany him to his study for a preliminary briefing. He sat down at his desk in a huge swivel chair and motioned to her to sit opposite.

Franz Hucke was a large, rotund man with a bushy moustache. She had been amused that when speaking of him, Lotta had always referred to him as Herr Hucke, never as her husband or Franz. Apparently, he was the town burgomaster. That meant that he had certain privileges that he was able to use to his advantage. Just as she was wondering how he and Lotta came to be involved in the resistance movement, he cut across her thoughts.

"Perhaps, Fräulein, you wonder why we are working with British intelligence and the French Resistance. Make no mistake—we love our country, but we don't like what has been happening here in Germany since the rise to power of the National Socialists. Some of us who don't support them feel we must take an active part in opposing fascism. There has been a resistance movement here for many years. We come from all walks of life and some members of our group, like Otto, are Communists. You probably know that the Fascists hate Communists almost as much as they do Jews.

"Otto joined us early in nineteen thirty-nine. He was against the pact which Russia made with Germany in the early part of the war. Now Russia is on the side of the Allies." Herr Hucke paused for a while, as though considering how best to proceed.

"I'm sure you understand," he said, "that all of us in the group are dependent on each other for our lives, and that includes many members of the French Resistance who are working with us. You have been sent to do a very important job. In the identity of Hildegard Hessler, we have a perfect cover for you. There was no one in our group here who matched her description as well as you and who would have been suitable for this mission."

She'd been wondering about this. Why couldn't they have found someone in the movement who was already living in Germany? Herr Hucke was at last offering an explanation.

He went on: "Even if there had been anyone, her real identity might have been discovered at some time, whereas you have no traceable past here. Apart from speaking fluent German and having the right appearance and background, I understand that you also speak several other languages fluently. This will enable you to pose as an official interpreter, but my wife will explain more about that later."

He twisted his large frame in the chair as though trying to get comfortable.

"You should have been told, before you took on this assignment, that you are required to get to know a certain colonel in the Wehrmacht who is working at headquarters in Berlin. His name is Karl von Richter."

"Yes," she said, "I was briefed by an officer in British intelligence. I know that this man is involved in troop movements and is now working with the German intelligence service in Berlin."

"Have you been acquainted with his personal details?"
asked Herr Hucke.

"I know that he is thirty-seven, a widower, has a young daughter who is ten, and that he was wounded and decorated for bravery on two occasions."

"That's right," he said, "but I can tell you more about him. Apart from a family home near to the Swiss border, he has a house south-west of Berlin, where his daughter has lived since the death of his wife. It is there that he holds frequent meetings with other high-ranking officers and officials."

Herr Hucke eased himself around in his chair again. "Your assignment is a long-term one," he said. "Your aim initially will be to get to know the colonel and try to gain his trust and confidence. It is said that he has a reputation with the ladies, so that may make your task easier. I'm sure you will know how best to go about it. You must try to find out as much as you can about him. We want to plant someone at the house where he holds the meetings, and we are hoping it will be you. However, if you're not successful in capturing the colonel's interest, which would surprise me, it may help if you can find out what staff he has there."

"I'm wondering how and where I shall be able to meet him, Herr Hucke."

"That will be easy. I'll explain in a moment," he said. "We know that all this may take some time to achieve. It is important that you do nothing to jeopardise your position in the early stages, so we do not want you to feel under pressure. Your time to serve the Resistance could come much later."

Herr Hucke was hesitating and appeared somewhat uncomfortable after explaining her assignment more fully. She realised that she was being used as bait to trap von Richter and that Herr Hucke would take it for granted that she had volunteered for the assignment.

"I hope, Fräulein, that you have been taught how to use a handgun."

"Yes, I have," she assured him.

"Good," he said, nodding his head several times, "but I do not think it would be wise for you to carry a weapon at this stage. Later, if and when the occasion arises, I will provide you with one."

He continued, "A reception is to be held in Berlin, to which I, as an official, will be invited along with Frau Hucke. I shall request an invitation for you to attend because Colonel von Richter will almost certainly be there. I have met him before on similar occasions, so I shall be able to introduce you. Then it will be up to you.

Remember that if you tell him that you are an interpreter and speak several languages, it could be useful." Herr Hucke rose to his feet. "We can talk many times before you meet him. Now, Fräulein, I will leave you with Lotta.

She will have much to tell you."

"Thank you, Herr Hucke, but please call me Hildegard—I need to get used to people calling me by that name."

"You're right. I shall make a point of it."

Herr Hucke had told her that he led the group, that instructions would come from him, and that she must report to him. He was extremely formal, and to a lesser extent, Lotta was too. They were both very thorough, however, and Hildegard was appreciative of this, but her relations with them were cool. She missed the comradeship she'd had with her contacts in France. *On reflection, though, it may be best this way,* she thought. She was here to do a job, to become a spy, even an assassin if the need arose, so perhaps formality was best in this situation. It might be unwise to become too close to members of the group.

She found Lotta in the sitting room. "Herr Hucke has finished with me for now," she said.

"Good," said Lotta. "We can start with your clothes. You will need new clothes for the part you will be playing."

"I was not given much money when I left England," Hildegard explained, "but I was told that money would be made available to me."

"There is no need for you to worry about that," Lotta assured her. "We have funds and shall be able to pass on ample money for your needs. Everything has been taken care of."

"Surely clothes are in short supply?"

"Yes," replied Lotta, "but there is the black market.

Also, as I am Swiss born, I can go into Switzerland without much difficulty. Your new identity papers show your mother to have been Swiss, so I think we can arrange for you to travel to

Switzerland. My sister lives there, so if I accompany you, there should be no problem. She will be able to help us find clothes for you. It is also important for you to meet with our Swiss agent so that we can establish a contact for you in Switzerland. If you claim to be an interpreter, we think it could perhaps become a useful cover for you in the future. I shall make the necessary arrangements for us to travel as soon as possible."

Lotta was so efficient and meticulous to detail in organising everything for her that Hildegard couldn't help feeling that she was being pushed along too quickly and that things were out of her control. Nevertheless, she was grateful to Lotta because she knew that she would soon have to work alone, and all the careful preparation and attention to detail could be of vital importance.

Everything went as Lotta had expected. They visited Switzerland and were able to carry out their plans.

Hildegard also discovered that many things were available in Germany on the black market, which was flourishing and provided well for those who could afford it.

One day, after they had returned to Germany, Lotta announced that she wanted to talk to her about personal matters concerning her health and that she had arranged for her to see a doctor for her protection. Hildegard realised what she meant and explained that all such matters had been taken care of before she left England. Nevertheless, Lotta insisted that she visit the German doctor, so Hildegard dutifully agreed, knowing that Lotta had her best interests in mind.

Finally she was taken to see the place where Hildegard Hessler had lived. To enable Hildegard to become familiar with her background, Lotta decided they should stay in the area for a day or two. Together they walked around the small town, visiting the public buildings and one or two of the older shops. They also went to see the house where the real Hildegard Hessler was born and the church and infant school which she would almost certainly have attended.

When they returned, Hildegard had several sessions with Herr Hucke, who patiently answered her many questions before telling her that he had obtained the invitation for her to attend the reception. All arrangements had been made, so when the day came, she travelled with Lotta and Franz Hucke to Berlin, where he had booked rooms for an overnight stay at a small hotel called the Hotel Meisler.

The reception was held in a building located in one of the main squares in the city centre. When they arrived, she saw that there were both Wehrmacht and Luftwaffe senior personnel as well as civilians present. Some, like Herr Hucke, were no doubt town officials who'd brought their wives. She was looking around wondering if Colonel von Richter was among those present when Herr Hucke whispered to her.

"Von Richter has just entered the room and is talking to a small group to the right of the main doors. Come—we will go across to the buffet, and then in a few minutes, I will take you over and introduce you."

She stole a glance in the direction Herr Hucke had indicated and saw a group of people, one of whom was a colonel; this was obviously the man they wanted her to seduce. That's when the colonel looked across the room and caught her glance. At that point, their eyes met, and she felt the pulse in her neck throbbing. She looked away quickly. She thought that he was without doubt, a very handsome man. He was tall, with blond hair, a fresh complexion and ruggedly attractive features. She chanced another glance in his direction and found that he was still looking her way. At that point, he smiled and gave her a cross between a nod and bow. She managed a smile in return before looking away again.

A tall glamorous woman standing nearby had noticed this. "Handsome, isn't he?" she said. "I can guarantee that half the women in the room have been waiting for his arrival, and he knows it. Perhaps you are the favoured one tonight."

Hildegard smiled and mumbled something in reply. She would obviously have to face some competition. She was still trying to compose herself and was considering why his glance had fallen upon her when Herr Hucke took her elbow and gently ushered her across the room to where the colonel was standing.

"Good evening, Colonel von Richter. You perhaps remember me—we met before at a similar reception," said Herr Hucke, beaming.

The colonel looked at him vaguely.

"May I introduce Fräulein Hildegard Hessler, my wife's niece, or perhaps I should say my wife's friend whom she regards as her niece."

"I am honoured," the colonel said, giving her another bow. He clearly had no recollection of meeting Herr Hucke, who was beginning to look uncomfortable.

Instead, he directed his attention to Hildegard, so at that point, Herr Hucke decided it would be best to make his exit.

"Please excuse me. I have left my wife with a friend, and I should escort them to the buffet," he said.

With that, he moved away, leaving Hildegard and the colonel together. The colonel smiled at her.

"For how long will you be staying in Berlin, Fräulein?" he enquired.

She still felt flustered but fought to conceal it. "I am not sure whether Herr Hucke has reserved our rooms at the Hotel Meisler for more than one night."

"It would be a pity if you have to leave Berlin so soon.

I was hoping you might agree to have lunch with me tomorrow."

"That is most kind of you, Colonel," she replied. "I feel sure it would be all right—I could always catch a later train if Herr Hucke and my aunt wish to return early tomorrow."

"Good. I will call for you at your hotel, then, at around noon. Now I must ask you to forgive me—regrettably, I am unable to stay for long and should apologise to our host before I leave. I shall look forward to tomorrow, Fräulein," he said, giving her a final bow.

By now, she was concerned that she might have appeared too eager, but she reminded herself that it was her job to get to know this man and that she had been given an unexpected opportunity to do so without much difficulty. When she reported to Herr Hucke, he expressed his satisfaction with her progress.

"We could not have hoped for more," he said. "You must stay on in Berlin for longer if things are going well."

Lotta and her husband did catch an early train the next morning. Hildegard was left to anticipate the meeting with Colonel von Richter. She had to admit to her growing excitement being a little more than a desire to get on with her job. She had a leisurely bath and took much of the morning getting ready for the meeting, wishing that she had brought more suitable clothes with her. Although the dress she would be wearing was pretty, she would like to have worn something that gave her a more sophisticated appearance.

At twelve o'clock precisely, the hotel porter knocked on her door to tell her that Colonel von Richter had arrived. She slowly collected her bag, threw her coat over her arm, and took a few deep breaths in an effort to remain calm before descending the two flights of stairs to the ground floor.

The colonel was standing in the reception hall and came forward. His eyes rested upon her.

"How delightful you look, Fräulein."

"Thank you," she said, "but please, Colonel, call me Hildegard."

"Only if you call me Karl," he replied.

She smiled shyly, feeling that she was behaving like a schoolgirl rather than an experienced woman. She did not know that it was her naturalness and lack of sophistication that delighted him.

The Hotel Meisler didn't serve lunch, so he took her to a small privately owned hotel where the proprietor seemed to know him.

"I have reserved a table in the corner by the window for you, Herr Colonel," he told him.

As the meal progressed, she felt more at ease and was enjoying the colonel's company. She found him charming, and he didn't try to impress her or talk down to her, as she had feared he might have done. On one occasion, she knew that he'd noticed her looking at his hands. They were big hands with long tapering fingers, and she wondered if he knew that women look at the hands of men they are considering as possible lovers.

"This is pleasant. I am enjoying it so much," she ventured with a smile.

"So am I," he said convincingly.

When they finished the meal, the waiter suggested that they might like coffee and drinks in the lounge. It turned out to be a room on the first floor, and as it happened, it was at that time unoccupied. The waiter placed their drinks on a low table in front of the settee where they sat side by side, and when the waiter left, Karl gently turned her head towards him and kissed her. Her heart was beating loudly, and she felt he must surely hear it.

"Thank you for coming to lunch with me today, Hildegard," he said. "Once again, I shall have to cut our meeting short. Will you stay another night at your hotel and have dinner with me tomorrow, when I'll have more time?"

"Yes, Karl, I'd like that very much," she said, "but I haven't brought any other clothes with me."

"Come just as you are now," he replied, smiling at her.

When she was back at the Hotel Meisler, she told herself once again that she was only doing her job, but secretly she knew that there was more to it than that. She felt a sense of excitement that she could not explain and continued to reason with herself that there was nothing wrong in finding him attractive so long as she behaved sensibly and kept her objective in mind.

When the next day came, time dragged. She decided to wear the dress that she had worn at the reception because it gave her more confidence. She was determined not to give him the impression that his pursuit of her would be easy, in case he soon tired of her. She had to keep his interest in her alive; otherwise, her job might become impossible. Her problem was in finding the right balance between giving him sufficient encouragement yet not appearing too eager.

When the time came for their rendezvous, she found the colonel waiting for her again.

"Hildegard, my dear," he said, putting an arm around her shoulders, "would you like to have dinner where we ate yesterday or perhaps you prefer a larger restaurant?"

"Oh, I think the hotel would be nicer," she said.

He seemed pleased. She had to admit that she liked the intimacy of the small hotel and wondered if they would be alone together in the lounge again.

The proprietor seated them in the corner by the window where they had sat the day before, and when he had ordered their food, Karl suddenly asked, "Is there no man in your life, Hildegard?"

The suddenness of the question took her by surprise. "No," she said simply. "There has not been anyone since the man I was engaged to was killed, nearly a year ago now."

"Army?"

"No, no, Luftwaffe," she replied. "His plane was shot down. And you?" she asked, already knowing his background.

"I have not been seriously involved with a woman since my wife was killed, and that was over two years ago."

"Was she killed in a bombing raid?"

"She was killed in a car accident," he said, "and I have a young daughter who is eleven years old now."

They talked for a while after the meal was over, and he told her about his house that was located on the outskirts of a pleasant village halfway between Berlin and the family home. It enabled him to visit his daughter more frequently than if she had remained at the family home. Fortunately, he had been successful in finding a good housekeeper and a governess to look after her. The housekeeper had taken on adequate staff to maintain the house and gardens.

Obviously he's very fond of his daughter, Hildegard thought. Conversation between them was easy, and time passed quickly. Then, just as they were about to go to the hotel lounge again, the loud wailing of an air raid siren startled them.

"Damn," he said angrily. "It has been some time since we had an air raid over Berlin. I think it would be best if you came back with me, Hildegard. I have a basement room for use in the event of air raids. It would be safer for you there than in the hotel. That is, if you agree?"

She agreed readily. "I have been lucky to avoid air raids so far. I would much prefer to be with you than at the hotel with people I don't know."

"Good, come along then—we must hurry," he said.

In one of the city squares, he took her to the building where his office and quarters were located. As they entered, a guard saluted, and the colonel spoke to a sergeant, who inspected Hildegard's papers. The colonel then led the way down some stairs to a basement room in which there was a desk and chair, a table and some sort of cupboard, as well as a sofa and a single bed. He invited her to be seated and went over to the cupboard, from which he took a bottle of cognac and glasses. They sat on the sofa together sipping the cognac and listening for the planes, but although an all-clear siren had not yet sounded, they could hear nothing. He put an arm around her, and they sat in silence for some time until Hildegard fell asleep, tired from the excitement and events of the day.

She awoke to the sound of a siren and found that she had her head on his shoulder. She straightened up. "What time is it?" she asked anxiously.

"It's just after midnight. I think you had better stay here tonight. It is likely that a second raid will follow."

"What do you think happened?" she asked.

"It could have been a false alarm, but it was more likely a first flight of planes which turned back for some reason." He looked at her. "You are tired," he said. "I will sleep on the sofa here, and you can have the bed. I will see if I can find something for you to wear."

He went to the cupboard and came back with a pair of pyjamas and a dressing gown.

"This is all there is, so you have the pyjama jacket and the dressing gown. If you take off your dress, I will hang it up. Let me know when you are ready," he said, turning the wooden chair to face the wall opposite and sitting down on it.

He had taken off his jacket, and when she saw him sitting there with his back to her, he didn't look like a German army colonel anymore. He was just a man. A man with whom she now knew she was falling in love. She was afraid and wanted human love and comfort, and at that moment, she gave in to temptation. She took off her clothes, but instead of putting on the jacket and getting into the bed, she lay on top of it. After a minute or two, he asked if she was ready.

"Yes, Karl, I'm ready," she replied.

He turned round to find her lying naked on the bed.

"Oh, Hildegard," he said, "I did not intend . . ."

"I know that," she said, "but don't you want me?"

He looked down at her. "I want you very much,"

he said, "but I wouldn't want to take advantage of the situation we are in."

She could not believe it was her own voice: "You are not; it's what I want."

A few moments later, he was lying on the bed beside her. Being together seemed so right, and when he made love to her, he was both passionate and gentle, as she had known he would be. Afterwards, she fell asleep in his arms.

An hour or so later, she awoke with a start to the sound of the warning siren once more.

"It's all right," he whispered, "I will not leave you."

This time, they could hear the planes overhead and the bombs dropping. Each time, the explosions grew louder, and she clung to him, shivering in his arms.

"Try not to be afraid, Hildegard," he said gently. "We are reasonably safe down here."

She thought of the planes overhead, British bombers probably, manned by frightened young men. Philip might so easily have been one of them had he lived. As well as the explosions, she could hear the rumbling of the German guns and wondered how many planes would return home to England that night. Many innocent German women and children might also be killed or injured.

Hildegard couldn't stop trembling but wasn't sure whether to attribute this to fear or excitement. She had come prepared to die but not prepared to fall in love. *I must regain control,* she thought, resolving that she would never let the love she felt for this man interfere with the job she had been sent to do. She had to remember all the people who had already risked their lives to help her. Meanwhile, the planes overhead were continuing to come in droves, and after the last ones had passed over, it was a long time before the all-clear siren sounded.

When at last this happened and she had stopped trembling, she was able to tell Karl that she was feeling much better. She preferred him to think that her trembling had been just due to her fear and not for any other reason. Karl said he would drive around to see the extent of the damage, and when he came back, he would arrange transport for her.

As soon as he had gone, she dressed and sat on the settee, awaiting his return. By now, she was feeling embarrassed and didn't know quite how to behave or what to say to him when he returned. Half an hour later, he came back, and when she saw him in his uniform once more, it served to remind her that he was, after all, a German army colonel.

He had gone to the other side of the room and was standing by the desk. "Most of the damage is in the residential area," he said, "but the station is intact and the trains are running, so I have asked my driver to take you to your hotel to collect your things and then to take you to the station."

She stood up. "Thank you, Colonel," she said.

At that, he strode across the room and took her by the shoulders. "Hildegard, what are you saying? We make love, you lay trembling in my arms for much of the night, and now you call me Colonel!"

She looked up at him. He looked stern. "I'm sorry, Karl," she said. "I am so confused. Everything seems to be happening to me at the same time." This was all true, of course.

His voice was gentle now. "Yes, I know. Believe me, if our country had not been at war I might have taken up to six months to court you, but as things are, we have to take what we can when we can. We have to live for the present because our future may be no more than the next day or the next week."

"But I feel so ashamed," she said. "Whatever must you think of me?"

"Hildegard, do you imagine that I would not have engineered it so that we made love the next time we met or, if not then, the time after that? But I would rather it had happened at a time when you were not afraid," he said. "As to what I think of you—you are a lovely young woman so please stop worrying and tell me when you next expect to be in Berlin again."

"It may be two or three weeks before I am back here,"

she said, not quite sure what to say.

"As soon as you come back, promise me that you will contact me, and I will arrange for you to stay in a hotel outside the city, where you will be safer from air raids."

"Yes, Karl," she said, "I promise." She was not used to anyone being so concerned about her welfare.

"If I don't hear from you within the next three weeks, I shall come looking for you, Hildegard," he warned. "Now I must go again. Come along. I will place you in the care of my sergeant."

In the train on the way back to the home of Herr Hucke and his wife, Hildegard sat thinking about her meetings with Karl von Richter. *How could I have been so naive as to fall in love with the man? she thought. I am certainly no femme fatale.* She had been set up for her part, but so had he; they were both vulnerable. British intelligence and German Resistance had done their job well, but they couldn't plan for the vagaries of the human heart. She decided not to tell Herr Hucke and Lotta the extent to which her relationship with the colonel had developed, but only that he expected to see her again in the next three weeks and was showing considerable interest. When she reported to them, both Lotta and Herr Hucke expressed their satisfaction with her further progress and encouraged her to plan a return visit to Berlin as soon as she felt a suitable amount of time had elapsed.

Lotta made arrangements with her sister for Hildegard to visit Switzerland again, as it was early in her relationship with the colonel and he might yet check up on her. In any event, Lotta thought that a short respite would help pass the time. Consequently, Hildegard was able to tell Karl that her services as an interpreter had been required in Switzerland and that she was travelling back home via Berlin.

It had been broadcast that there had been further bombing raids over Berlin, and she had been worried for Karl's safety, so as soon as she arrived, she made contact and was thankful to hear his voice. He'd booked a room for her in a hotel outside the town, as he had said he would, and arranged to visit her the following morning, explaining that he had weekend leave. As on previous occasions, he arrived on time for them to lunch together.

Hildegard was nervous about the meeting—it was two weeks since he had seen her, and she was not certain what his attitude towards her might be. She remembered what the glamorous woman at the reception had said when she first saw Karl and wondered if she would still be the favoured one... and for how long. She thought that he did seem pleased to see her, however.

When they were seated in the hotel restaurant, Karl leaned across the table. "I have looked forward to our meeting again, Hildegard," he said, smiling. "It is nice that we can be together without air raids overhead."

"Yes, it is. I heard that there had been more raids over Berlin, and I've been thinking about you and hoping you were safe. It's good to see you again, Karl."

His vivid blue eyes focused on her. "There's something I want to ask you," he said. "As I have three days' leave, I'm going home to see my daughter. I believe I told you that I visit her as often as I can. It would make me very happy if you would agree to be my guest and come with me. I think you would like the house, and I should like you to meet my daughter as well."

This would be an excellent chance to learn more about him and to establish a relationship for the future, she thought. Apart from that, there was nothing she wanted more than to be with him again. She pretended to hesitate.

"Please come, Hildegard," he said.

"I'd be delighted to accept your invitation," she said quietly.

They set out together for his home, located near a small village south west of Berlin. When at last they turned from the road into a wide driveway and the house came into view, Hildegard saw that it was old and full of character. She had expected it to be smaller, because she thought Karl's main reason for buying it was to provide a home for his daughter which was safe but nearer to Berlin than the family home. Later she learned that he had inherited the family home and that it was considerably larger than the one they were visiting. Apparently, he'd lived there with his wife and daughter, Elsa, before the war.

While Karl was collecting her suitcase, she stood looking at the front of the house and the approach to it. There were lawns bordered by many varieties of shrubs, some of which were in flower, and a wide stone path led from the driveway to the front entrance. She thought the house had a welcoming look about it. She didn't know then how much the house would feature in her life or that she would return to it repeatedly, sometimes with a heavy heart and at other times with great happiness.

"I'll go in search of Frau Becker," he said, as they went inside. Just then, a woman of about forty years, small and rather plump, came hurrying from one of the rooms, and Karl introduced her as his housekeeper, Frieda Becker. She smiled broadly at Hildegard in welcome.

"Fräulein Hessler will be staying with us for a few days," he said, "so will you please prepare one of the guest rooms for her?"

He turned to Hildegard. "As well as running the household, Frau Becker is also a very good cook."

Frau Becker looked pleased as she went off to get Hildegard's room ready.

Later Karl introduced her to the other resident staff, which included Frau Becker's husband, Hans, who acted as chauffeur, and Elsa's governess, referred to as "the Fräulein". There was also Schultz, the gardener. All had rooms on the second floor of the house, as did Elsa, whose room was next to the Fräulein's. It turned out that apart from the bedrooms, on the same floor were a sitting room, a small kitchen, and the schoolroom where Elsa took her lessons. On the first floor were Karl's room, three guest rooms, a sitting room, and a small dining room.

Frau Becker took her to the guest room next to Karl's room, and she learned that there were no other guests staying at the house but her. When Hildegard returned, Karl showed her around some of the rooms on the ground floor. First they went into a large room which was comfortably furnished, with many paintings hanging on the walls. He saw her looking at some of them and took her by the arm, walking her over to a portrait of a young woman with long golden hair and wearing a red velvet ball gown.

"Does she remind you of someone?" he asked.

Hildegard studied the painting. "She's beautiful," she said, "but I cannot say I recognise her as looking like anyone I know. Who is she?"

"She's my grandmother," said Karl. Then he took her by the arm again and walked her over to a long side table above which hung a large mirror.

"Now does she remind you of anyone?" he asked.

"You don't mean me?" she said incredulously.

"I do," he said. "From the moment I first saw you, I was struck by your likeness to her."

"I'm flattered," she said, wanting to laugh aloud. *So he believes I look like his grandmother!* Instead, she just smiled, for she was now sure that he was genuinely attracted to her. She knew that with her blond hair and blue eyes, she was the Nazi idea of ideal womanhood. They thought all blue-eyed blond men and women were of pure Aryan blood and were therefore superior. She remembered Karl's kindness to her, though, and how considerate he had been, and she felt that she had to weigh one possibility against another. *Perhaps that's how it will always be with our relationship*, she thought.

Continuing their tour around the house, he took her to a room he called his study, which was also a library, except that one wall was dedicated to miniature paintings. She later learned that Karl had a passion for all things small, and that included women. Finally they went to the dining room, which had heavy furnishings and housed a huge table. *This must be where he holds the meetings with the other senior officers and officials,* she concluded.

"Elsa's lessons with the Fräulein finish at about four o' clock, and when I'm home, she usually joins me in the sitting room upstairs," he said. "We then spend the rest of the day together until she goes off to bed at about eight." He looked at his watch. "It is time for you to meet her, I think."

They went to the first-floor sitting room, and it was not long before Elsa joined them, rushing up to her father and hugging him. Karl introduced Hildegard as his friend. Elsa looked delighted. Karl explained that she loved having visitors to the house. Soon Elsa was asking her father if she could take Hildegard for a walk to the village the next morning.

Karl grinned. "Well, first we had better ask her if she would like to go to the village."

"I should like that very much," said Hildegard.

"I'll show you where the Fräulein and I sometimes go to do shopping for Frau Becker," said Elsa.

Hildegard smiled at Karl. Elsa seemed a delightful child.

Later, after dinner, when she and Karl were alone together, he said, "You seem to be a success with Elsa."

"Is she always so friendly as soon as she meets someone?"

Hildegard enquired.

"Not always, but she obviously likes you."

"I'm so glad. I like her too, and I think we shall get on well together," said Hildegard, and she meant it. She then wandered over to the grand piano which stood at the end of the sitting room. "Do you play the piano?" she asked.

"Yes, I shall play for you tomorrow if you wish, but for now come over here and sit with me."

She sat down beside him. "After Berlin, it seems so quiet here," she said as he put his arm around her.

He was smiling. "Frau Becker has given you the room next to my own," said Karl. "I hope you will find it comfortable."

"Yes, I am certain I shall," she assured him.

"I will only visit you in your room if I am invited to do so, you know," he said after a while.

"It's a lovely room, but I do think that I may feel a little lonely there on my own," she teased.

"Well, I wouldn't want you to feel lonely, so perhaps I had better remedy that—what do you think?"

She laughed. "Yes, I think that is a good idea."

"That's settled then." He turned her face to his and gently kissed both eyelids before kissing her lips.

No man had ever done that before, and at that moment, she felt an overwhelming love for him. She knew that a net was being drawn ever tighter around her, from which there was no escape.

The next two days passed swiftly. During the day, Hildegard divided her time between Elsa and Karl, and sometimes they all played in the garden with Wrex, the family dog. Wrex was a German shepherd dog and followed Karl around whenever he could.

The evening before they were due to leave, Hildegard and Karl strolled in the garden together. It was a warm evening, and they went down the long path to a stream that ran along the bottom of the garden. They sat on a seat there. The scent of evening primrose was in the air, and around the seat grew wild forget-me-nots, still in flower following a late start to spring. She thought it one of the most beautiful gardens she had seen.

"I love this place. I feel at peace when I come home here," Karl said. "You know, Hildegard, if you lived here, you would not need to stop off in Berlin whenever you broke your journey, and you would be safer here. You would not have to give up your job as an interpreter, and you could easily visit your aunt whenever you wanted. I can see that Elsa is already becoming fond of you, and perhaps if you lived here, you might consider providing her with a little extra tuition in English and French. Do you understand what I am asking you?"

"Yes, of course. You are suggesting I come to live here."

"Well, a little more than that. I am asking you to live with me openly, without the pretence of separate rooms." Hildegard knew that she would accept. This was what the movement had hoped for; it was the purpose of their plans, but she knew also that she would have accepted his offer anyway.

"I don't expect your answer now," Karl said. "Think about it and tell me tomorrow."

"Karl, dear Karl, you must know that my answer will be yes," she said.

"There is so much more that I should like to offer you. Sadly, I cannot do so at this time, but if you agree to come to me, I shall look after you just the same."

She was not entirely sure what he meant by that but decided not to pursue it.

Before they parted the next day, they made plans for her to move in at the commencement of Karl's leave the following month, and he said that he would explain the situation to Elsa and Frau Becker before then. When Elsa came to say goodbye, she asked Hildegard when she would be coming again. "Probably quite soon," Hildegard replied, wondering how Elsa would react when Karl told her that she would be moving in with him. She hoped it wouldn't be too much of a shock for the child—she didn't want to appear to be trying to take her mother's place.

Back once more with Herr Hucke and Lotta, Hildegard related the story of her visit to Colonel von Richter's home, but she still kept secret the real relationship she had with him. Instead, she told them that he had asked her to give his daughter extra tuition in languages and she had agreed, providing he allowed her to retain her job as an interpreter and to visit Lotta occasionally. Yet again, they expressed their satisfaction at the way it had worked out.

During the following weeks, various plans were made for the move. Lotta was busy arranging for funds to be transferred to the bank nearest to where Hildegard would be living so that money would always be available for her needs, and Herr Hucke arranged for a female agent to move into rooms in the village near the colonel's home.

"We're hoping that she will be able to obtain a job in one of the shops in the village," he told her. "This will enable you to pass messages to her for Otto, should you be unable to contact Lotta."

They agreed that initially she would report to Herr Hucke by making regular monthly visits to her aunt. Before she left, Herr Hucke briefed Hildegard as to what information they needed. However, he made it clear that she was to take no risks now, as it was more important for her to establish her position. Arrangements were made for her luggage to be sent ahead, and on the appointed day, she took a train to the nearest station, where she was met by the housekeeper's husband, Hans Becker, who drove her to Karl's home.

Thus it was on a summer's day in 1942 that Alice Grant, now Hildegard Hessler, moved into the home of Colonel von Richter and commenced her life as a spy and also as the colonel's lady, a role she much preferred.

Chapter 5

HALCYON DAYS

When she first arrived at Karl von Richter's house, Hildegard was worried about the reception she might receive from the other members of the household. She wanted at all costs to avoid making enemies. Her concern was that Frau Becker might see her own role as threatened, and that Elsa might feel resentful and think of her as a rival for her father's affections.

Fortunately, both these fears proved groundless. From the beginning, Frau Becker had taken great care to make her feel welcome, even redoing Karl's room to give it more feminine appeal by bringing in different furniture and floral covers and curtains from the guest rooms. Hildegard soon learned that Frau Becker was extremely loyal to the colonel. She always did whatever she could to ensure his comfort and happiness—and Hildegard's too, when she became his lady.

Karl's two weeks of leave were ending, and the following day he would be returning to Berlin. There was now no doubt in Hildegard's mind that she truly loved him and would be anxiously awaiting his next visit. That night as she sat at the dressing table brushing her hair, she saw in the mirror that Karl was watching her. She hoped that he hadn't seen the tears that escaped and ran down her cheeks. Quickly she wiped them away with the back of her hand. She was both happy and sad. Happy to be with him and sad because she knew the relationship was doomed. She wondered which of them would end up destroying the other.

Karl was smiling; he had been looking at her reflection in the mirror. She would have been pleased had she known that he was thinking what a pretty little thing she was and how lucky he was to have found her. She turned round to face him and met his eyes. Deciding for now to live only for the present, she smiled at him before running across the room to climb into the bed beside him.

After Karl returned to Berlin, it seemed strange at first. She still had to get used to living in his house without him. There was little she could do just yet as far as spying activities, but the group had accepted this. Meanwhile, she just enjoyed the comfort and tranquillity of the house and garden.

The garden was a real delight to her. There was a long winding pathway through the flowerbeds and lawns, and she would often stroll down to the stream and sit on the seat there. She and Elsa sometimes paddled with the dog. At other times, at Elsa's request, they would have a picnic lunch in the nearby summerhouse.

One morning when Elsa was working at her lessons with the Fräulein, Hildegard strolled into the woods.

These adjoined the garden and seemed to her to be part of it. At first, she was able to follow a wide track, but then the undergrowth became too dense. She decided to turn back. Before doing so, however, she was able to see what looked like a small clearing ahead, so she walked a little farther. As she came to the clearing, a heavenly scent filled the air. She couldn't identify it at first but then looked down and recognised the camomile plants which formed a soft green carpet at her feet. It was so lovely that she wondered whether it had been part of a cultivated garden at some point. She made up her mind to bring Karl there one day.

Now that she was living in Germany, she began to think more and more about her mother, remembering some of the things they had done together in her childhood. Even though her mother had died years ago, she still missed her. She knew that she had been born in Leipzig, and planned to go there one day. Her mother would have understood about her falling in love with Karl because she herself had fallen in love with and married a man of a different nationality. But Hildegard knew that her mother would have been loyal to the man she loved, whereas she was not.

When war was declared, many Germans living in England were rounded up and confined to prison camps. She wondered if that would have been her mother's fate had she lived. *It's just as well that she had no relatives alive here now,* she thought. Her grandparents had both died by the time her parents brought her to live in Germany as a child. Hildegard vaguely remembered an uncle. She believed he too had died before her parents returned to England.

During the weeks that followed, Karl's visits were few, and he usually only stayed for one or occasionally two nights before returning to Berlin the next day. In between his visits, she took the opportunity to keep her promise to tutor Elsa in English and French. She always tried to make the lessons fun for the child, leaving her to do her written work with the Fräulein. As a result, the activity soon became a pleasure for both of them. Like Hildegard, Elsa had a natural ability with languages, and she quickly benefited from the tuition. Hildegard soon realised that Elsa was becoming attached to her, especially when Elsa confessed that she didn't like the Fräulein. Maybe Elsa regarded Frau Becker as a substitute mother and had come to think of Hildegard as her friend.

Hildegard didn't really approve of the way Elsa was being brought up, insofar as her being sheltered from so many aspects of life. She thought that Elsa should have someone her own age with whom she could share her secrets. Of course, she said nothing to Karl about that.

They were enjoying a long hot, summer, so whenever she knew that Karl was coming, she would wait for him in the garden. He usually arrived early in the afternoon, while Elsa was still having lessons with the Fräulein. Sometimes he would change into a shirt and slacks before coming to greet her. She preferred it when he did, because to her his uniform was a symbol of conflict. When he arrived, she would run to meet him and throw her arms around him. He would lift her off the ground before putting her down and kissing her. They often then sat on the wooden seat by the stream, where earlier in the year the wild forget-me-nots had covered the ground. It was an idyllic time for her.

One day during the Indian summer, Karl said that he would have three days of leave the following weekend. The day he was due to arrive was hot and sunny, so after lunch she changed into her button-through cotton dress, put on her sandals, and went down to the stream. She was sitting on the seat when he took her by surprise, having arrived earlier than usual. She'd already decided that that day she would take him to the clearing where she had found the camomile plants, so a short while later, she suggested they take a walk in the woods. When they came to the end of the track, she grabbed his hand and led him there.

"Look," she said, sitting down on the ground and waving her hand to indicate the beauty and seclusion of the spot.

Karl stood smiling down at her. "I suspect," he said, as he sat down beside her, "that my lady wants me to make love to her out here."

She smiled at him shyly, knowing that he loved that look.

"Yes, I was right," he said as he unfastened her dress and saw that she was not wearing anything underneath. She took off the dress to use it as a groundsheet, and he removed his shirt, folded it, and placed it under her head. "There," he said, "now you have a pillow."

At that moment, they were startled by the sound of rustling in the undergrowth; it wasn't a bird but something much larger. They both jumped to their feet and she pulled on her dress.

"Whatever was that?" she asked.

"Occasionally wild animals stray into these parts. It may have been a boar. I think perhaps we should go back to the house, Hildegard, and up to our room," Karl said.

They did as he suggested, but when they reached the landing at the top of the stairs, they bumped into the Fräulein, who gave them a withering look of disdain. Karl spoke to her, and she mumbled something in reply before dashing down the stairs.

"I wonder what's wrong with her," he said.

As soon as they entered their room, Hildegard cried out in dismay, "Oh, Karl, that accounts for it. In my panic, I forgot to button my dress, so what with the sight of you bare-chested and me in this dishevelled state, it must have been a terrible shock for the poor Fräulein."

The thought of the look on the Fräulein's face was too much for both of them, and they collapsed on the bed together laughing. When their laughter subsided, they lay there in silence.

After a while, Karl turned to her. "I love you, Hildegard," he said. "You mean so much to me, and you have helped me regain some of my lost youth. The youth which I lost on the battlefields many years ago."

It was the first time he had actually said that he loved her, although she had felt it to be so. Her eyes filled with tears; her happiness was complete. Whatever the future might bring, she would remember this moment forever.

"My darling Karl," she whispered. "I am sure you know that I love you in return."

That same evening, she was due to meet Karl's cousin Max for the first time. He would only be staying for one night because he would be going to the family home to spend time with his mother. Karl had told her that, like his father and grandfather, Max had made a career in the army and was a major in the Wehrmacht. She was just a little nervous about meeting another member of the von Richter family because she was concerned that an interested stranger might more easily catch her out somehow.

In the evening, when she was trying to pick out something suitable to wear for the occasion, Karl came and stood behind her.

"Yes," he said, "you look lovely in that."

She knew that he wanted to show her off, so to please him Hildegard wore the dress she was about to discard.

Max was quite different from what she had expected.

He bore little resemblance to Karl, being smaller and with brown hair and eyes, but he did have the same charm and gallantry. When Karl introduced them, Max kissed her on both cheeks and then held her away from him.

"I can see why Karl might want to keep you hidden away from men like me," he said with a smile. "Not that any of us ever stood much chance with the girls when Karl was around."

"Nonsense," said Karl, "you always had your fair share of young women." He turned to Hildegard. "He has a new girlfriend nearly every time I see him."

Karl had warned her that Max was flirtatious, a fun man, but said she would like him. He was right. She was unsure at first but soon warmed to him. It was obvious that the bond between the two men was strong. Max joked a lot, but she could see that the family tradition of honour, respect for women, and service to the country was strong. She knew that Max had been on active service and may have fought under Rommel, as had Karl, but so far she had not been able to gain much information about his present activities. For now, however, she was happy just to enjoy his company, as Karl so clearly did.

Max had arrived after Elsa had gone to bed, so she had been excused from her lessons the next morning. When she saw Max at breakfast, she couldn't stop talking, and he indulged her good-humouredly.

"My Uncle Max always makes me laugh," Elsa confided. "He mimics the Fräulein, you know. I wish he would come and see us more often."

Hildegard laughed. "We all enjoy his company, don't we?" she said. She had no fears about Max now that she had met him, and she even looked forward to his visit next time.

After they had finished breakfast, Karl took Max to his study, and the two men were ensconced there for over an hour. Hildegard wished she could find an excuse to go into the room, but she was unable to think of anything convincing.

They said goodbye to Max after lunch, and Elsa went to the Fräulein for afternoon lessons. Karl and Hildegard spent the rest of their precious time together. They had just one more day left before he would be gone again, and as usual, time passed all too quickly.

After Karl left, although she had little information to pass on thus far, Hildegard felt that she must report to the Resistance and visit Lotta and Herr Hucke. So much had happened to her since her last visit, but hardly any of it had anything to do with her assignment. After she told them what little she could, they again both expressed their opinion that her opportunity to do more would come in the future. Herr Hucke told her that the agent was now working at the drapery shop in the village near to the colonel's home. Her name was Eva, and if necessary, she would be able to pass messages to Otto.

Hildegard returned home in better spirits, without feeling guilt about her lack of progress. She was thankful that the time when she might be required to start acting against Karl's interests was in the unforeseeable future.

At the weekend, when Elsa was free of lessons, Hildegard took her for a walk to the village, intending to teach her more English by getting her to name the shops and some of the goods they had for sale. Elsa had money to spend, so they went into the grocery store, which sold many other things beside groceries. The shopkeeper often put things that were in short supply, like coffee, tea, or cheese, to one side for Frau Becker, and that sometimes included chocolate for Elsa, so Hildegard went to collect whatever was available. From the moment she entered the shop, however, there was a hush, except for two women tittering. Somehow, she felt she had been the cause of the atmosphere and was glad that Elsa was busy searching through old picture postcards and appeared not to have noticed anything unusual.

When Hildegard returned, she related the incident to Frau Becker. She had begun to regard Frau Becker as a friend, and the two women were on first-name terms when they were alone together.

"I will go into the village myself tomorrow," said Frieda, "and try to get to the bottom of it. I have an idea what it might be about."

"What do you mean?" Hildegard enquired.

"Well," replied Frieda, "on the first day of the colonel's last visit, I believe you took a walk through the woods together. When you and the colonel go alone into the garden, I am usually able to divert Elsa's attention and prevent her from going there. On that occasion, I missed her, and she ran out with Wrex. It seems the dog tracked you into the woods and Elsa followed. She saw you together and unfortunately told the Fräulein that she had seen you sunbathing with no clothes on."

"Oh my goodness!" exclaimed Hildegard.

Frieda went on: "The Fräulein then saw you together on the stairs and lost no time coming to relate the whole thing to me."

"I'm really sorry that Elsa saw us. I won't let it happen again," Hildegard said apologetically, feeling embarrassed.

"Please don't worry," said Frieda. "Elsa should never have gone into the woods; her father has forbidden her to go there alone. I spoke to her and made her promise not to tell anyone else that she saw you. In return, I said that on this occasion, I would not tell her father that she was there. From what you have said, I suspect that the Fräulein may have been spreading gossip in the village. I shall feel obliged now to tell the colonel because I know that he would not want you to suffer such treatment. He will probably warn her against it; meanwhile, perhaps you might prefer to stay away from the village for a while."

"Thank you, Frieda," said Hildegard. "I am concerned, though."

"You really mustn't worry," said Frieda. "The Fräulein is a silly girl. She is jealous of you because she thought the colonel would have chosen her instead, but I could have told her that would never happen."

Hildegard didn't go into the village again until after Karl's next visit. He'd called the Fräulein to his study to tell her that if he found that anyone had been spreading gossip about any member of his household, that person would have to leave his employ.

After that, the incident appeared to be forgotten, but Hildegard was concerned. She knew that the Fräulein's jealousy could make her a dangerous enemy. From then on, she tried to think of ways in which she might make the Fräulein better disposed towards her. *Perhaps it would be a good idea to involve Elsa in some way,* she thought. Maybe they could all three take a trip to the nearest town for Elsa's birthday. She wondered if she should discuss it with Karl first. On the other hand, she was the colonel's lady now, and she could see no reason why he would object if she arranged an outing and included a member of the household.

Her opportunity came unexpectedly. One day when she was walking back from the village, Hildegard saw a notice outside the village hall. A visiting troupe of theatre players was to perform a classic play at the hall, and there would be a performance one afternoon. When Hildegard told them about it, Elsa was excited. The Fräulein just sniffed but agreed that Elsa should see the play because it would be educational for her.

Herr Becker would be bringing the car to collect them after the performance. As it was a fine day, they set out in the afternoon to walk to the village hall. Hildegard had decided that she would encourage the Fräulein to talk about herself, and this was the best time to do it.

"I cannot keep calling you 'Fräulein'," she said. "What's your name?"

The Fräulein looked nonplussed. "Ursula Fischer," she said.

"Then I shall call you Ursula... and 'Fräulein Ursula' when I am speaking of you to Elsa. Do you come from around here, Ursula?"

"My parents live in Hamburg, and I was brought up there, but my brother is in Berlin. He is in the SS," she said proudly. "He's been helping to clear the Jews out of Berlin and send them away to camps. The Führer says they would have taken over the country if we had let them. Klaus, that's my brother, has met the Führer and says what a wonderful man he is."

It came as a shock to Hildegard to hear anyone talking this way. At the house, she was hidden away from what was happening in the towns and cities. But she remembered what her instructor had told her before she left England—about thinking before she spoke and not showing her feelings.

"I can see that you are very proud of your brother," she said. "Do you manage to see him sometimes?"

"Well, not often. He seldom gets leave because his job is too important."

Hildegard was really struggling to make conversation now, so she changed the subject. They talked about Elsa's lessons. She felt that she'd made some headway. The Fräulein was at least talking to her, but she couldn't help wondering if Karl knew about the Fräulein's brother and, if so, whether or not he approved. She certainly hoped that the Fräulein didn't feed Nazi propaganda about the Jews to Elsa. She decided that she would tell Karl that she had taken them to the village to see the play and then drop it into the conversation that the Fräulein's brother was in the SS and see how he reacted.

It was early in December before Karl was able to get away again, but at least he had several days available. This time, he took Hildegard and Elsa to the family home to visit his Aunt Christa. She found it hard to believe that his aunt was Max's mother because she was so formal. When the elderly woman welcomed her, she said that Max had spoken much about her. Hildegard wondered how much she knew about her relationship with Karl and what she thought about that.

Karl showed her around his family home, which was big and imposing. Although comfortably furnished, it seemed a cold and unfriendly place in comparison to the house that he had bought for Elsa, where they now lived. Hildegard was particularly interested to see, in one of the rooms, a photograph of his wife and Elsa when she was a baby. His wife was an attractive woman, probably in her mid-twenties when the photograph was taken. It must have been a terrible shock for the family when she was killed. That it was the result of a car accident near to home must have made it worse.

Before they left, Aunt Christa called her to one side. "I should like to give you this," she said, handing her a gold locket and chain. "It belonged to Karl's mother. He has agreed that you should have it."

She explained that most of his mother's jewellery was left in trust for Elsa, but one or two items had passed to her. One of them was the locket. Hildegard was surprised about the gift because she thought Christa might have disapproved of her. She kissed the older woman.

"Thank you, Aunt Christa. I shall treasure it," she said, and was delighted when she found a picture of Karl on one side and one of Elsa, when she was about five years old, on the other.

Whenever something like this happened, Hildegard found it hard to bear because they accepted her as part of the family and were so innocent of what she really was. She didn't want to hurt any of them, as she feared she might have to one day.

The next day after dinner, when they were alone together in the sitting room, Karl talked about their visit to the family home.

"I am sure that Max will not want to live there after Aunt Christa dies," he said, "so I think I shall sell it then. You would prefer that we live here, wouldn't you?"

That he believed they would still be together should have made Hildegard happy, but it only made her sad. "I love this place; you know I do," she said, trying hard not to show the concern she felt about the future.

Karl returned to Berlin, and the weeks passed. Christmas came and he was able to get away again for a few days. Early on, he had explained to her that after he had been wounded a second time, he had been pronounced unfit for active service. That was the reason he had been moved to work at the headquarters in Berlin. The one good thing was that he had generous leave. She welcomed it, of course. But as the raids over Berlin were becoming heavier and more frequent, she knew that he was probably in as much danger there as he would have been on active service.

Chapter 6

DOWN TO WORK

Early in the January of 1943, Karl came home again. He told Hildegard that he must work for some of the time. But they would have free days which they could spend together. She had thought that the meetings of which Herr Hucke had spoken must be about to start and feared that their life together might never be the same again. It would mark the beginning of something new.

On the day Karl arrived, and after they had eaten in the evening, he sat down at the piano and began to play. He sang Schubert songs in his rich baritone voice. When he had finished, she went over and stood behind him.

“Thank you—that was lovely, darling,” she said, placing her hands on his shoulders. “Please play a little Mozart now.”

“Just for you,” he said, “and then I want to talk to you about the coming week.”

After that, Hildegard couldn’t listen to the music. Fear of the future was ever present. She watched him close the piano and stand up. Then she smiled as she looked up into the face that had become so dear to her. Her eyes brimmed with tears.

"You play so beautifully," she said. They moved away from the piano and sat down together on the sofa As he put his arm around her, she asked nervously, "What is it you want to tell me Karl?"

"We can spend the next two days together," he said, "but on Tuesday Max will be paying us a short visit again, and then a number of senior Wehrmacht and Luftwaffe personnel will be attending a meeting here on Thursday. They will stay on for dinner, so I shall be busy until late that day. We can have Friday together, but the following day I must return to Berlin. As Max will not be leaving until after the meeting has started on Thursday morning, I'm afraid I shall have to ask you to entertain him for much of the time. I hope you won't mind. I shall be busy preparing for the meeting for some part of the day before too."

"Oh, Karl, is that all? I like Max. It will be a pleasure, really."

"One other thing," he said, "I should like you and Elsa to keep to the rooms up here on Thursday until the men have left. Two of the day staff will be coming in to help Frau Becker with the dinner, so it will be no trouble for her if you eat up here separately."

"Yes, Karl," she said compliantly. She was puzzled, though. She wondered why she and Elsa shouldn't have a meal in the kitchen with Frau Becker and the Fräulein after Max had gone. She knew that Karl had always been protective of Elsa. She realised that he probably felt that he should also protect her in the same way. Hildegard didn't really understand this need for protection. However, she was glad that Max would be there for some of the time, because she really did enjoy his company and would look forward to his visit.

It was a cold winter's night, and a huge log fire was burning in the grate. The room was warm and comfortable. Hildegard put her head on Karl's shoulder, and they sat together in contented silence, listening to the occasional crackle of the fire.

"It is so good to be back home with you, Hilda," he said.

He had started to call her Hilda sometimes; it was his own special name for her. She snuggled up to him and wished she could hold these moments in time forever. She was afraid of change.

"Come on," he said. "I want to make love to you. Come to bed."

"I have a better idea," she told him, whispering in his ear. He kissed her and went over to put more logs on the fire while she piled cushions on the floor. They undressed and put out the light, making love in the glow of the firelight. Later that night she lay awake in bed wondering how she could reconcile her love for him with her duty to her country—but she could find no answer.

Two days later, Max arrived in his usual jovial mood. When Karl told him about the meeting, he grinned.

"What luck for me!" he said. "Do you mind if I take Hildegard and Elsa out to lunch tomorrow if you are working?"

"Despite your reputation, you are probably the only man to whom I would entrust them," Karl joked.

After their lunch with Max the next day, Elsa went for her afternoon lessons with the Fräulein. Hildegard was left alone with Max.

"I have never seen Karl so happy—not even when he was first married," he told her in a rare serious moment. "Sometimes Karl asks me why I have never married, and I must admit that I often wish I had, but sadly I never found the right girl. In a few months, I shall probably be put back on active service. At such times, I think how nice it would be to have someone back home here waiting for me."

She went over to him and kissed him on the cheek. "One day, Max, I am sure you will find someone special," she said.

"Someone like you, perhaps," he replied, smiling.

Later that afternoon, Karl joined them. All three sat laughing and joking after their evening meal. Later Hildegard left the room, and upon her return, when about to open the door, she overheard the two men talking seriously. She held back to listen.

"Things are not going well for Germany. I almost wish I too were going back on active service," she heard Karl say. "Before long it may be possible, but for now I have to continue with what I am doing. I cannot say that I enjoy it, but it is vital work."

"You think you will return to active service eventually?"

"Probably, but not until I am ordered to do so," Karl said. "I feel that while I can, I should stay behind to look after Elsa and Hildegard. I believe Hildegard would think that because she speaks English, she would be safe if the British or Americans or even the Russians occupied Germany. I doubt if she understands about men and war and what might happen to her."

"You don't really think it's going that badly, do you? You are talking as though we have lost the war."

"No, of course not," said Karl. "We'll turn it round again." There was a brief silence, and then she heard him say, "Should it happen that you survive and I do not, will you look after them for me?"

"You can rest assured of that," Max replied, "but you will survive, Karl. I am far more likely to be the one who does not."

At that point, she re-entered the room and the conversation was closed. The mood lightened, and Max amused them with army tales for the rest of the evening.

"Max has such a thirst for life," she said to Karl that night when they were alone, "but I wonder if the joking and laughter are to help him get through the war."

"Yes, very likely," he said. "We have to find ways of coping, and for Max it's by making light of his fears."

Hildegard continued to think about Max and how much he had in common with Marcel, even though they fought on opposite sides.

To her surprise, she learned the next day that the Fräulein and Herr Schultz were also confined to the upper rooms. *Why does Karl want to keep Schultz out of sight?* she wondered. She knew that Schultz had worked for him before at the family home, and she had often wondered if he was Jewish. Schultz might not be his real name. If he were Jewish, it might explain why he so seldom went out and why Karl wanted him out of the way while the meeting was taking place. What it did not explain, though, was Karl's reason for protecting him. Did he disapprove of the Nazi's attitude to the Jews, or was it for some quite different reason?

Hildegard had been unable to find out who attended the meeting, so there was no way that she could obtain information about what had taken place. Karl kept his papers in his study, no doubt locked away in his desk. That night, she noticed that he brought his briefcase into the bedroom.

She resolved that when Karl returned to Berlin, she would pay another visit to Herr Hucke to explain what had happened. Although she had achieved nothing, she was relieved that she still hadn't needed to betray Karl in any way. The conflict caused by the need to do her job and her desire not to harm him was always there.

Before Karl went, she told him that she would be visiting her aunt for a while. She didn't want him to return and find her gone without explanation. After he left, she walked into the village to establish contact with Eva, the agent Herr Hucke had mentioned on her last visit. He'd said she was working at the drapery shop. Fortunately, there was only one such shop in the village.

She found two women working behind the counter and decided to order something so that she could leave her name and address. When she left the shop Hildegard made a point of telling the assistant with whom she had placed her order that she had been very helpful, and that she would certainly come again. At that time, she had no idea which of the two women was the agent. Fortunately, the other assistant had overheard much of the conversation and noted that Hildegard had said she lived at the colonel's house. People in the village only seemed to know the house as "the colonel's house", including the mail carriers and deliverymen.

Hildegard smiled at the other assistant, who smiled back as she opened the door for her.

"My name is Eva," she said. "We shall look forward to seeing you again soon, Fräulein."

The two women showed no recognition of each other, but the necessary contact had been made for the future.

The next day, Hildegard spoke to Lotta. A visit was arranged, and a day or two later, she was reporting to Herr Hucke again. She told him about the meeting and about her lack of opportunity to obtain information.

"Yes, yes, I understand," said Herr Hucke. He sounded impatient this time.

"I must find a way of getting a key to the colonel's desk," she said. "He keeps it with a bunch of other keys which he carries with him. The best way would be if I could sedate him on the night after the meeting."

"So do you think you could put something in his drink?" Herr Hucke enquired.

"Yes, probably, but where would I obtain a suitable drug?"

Herr Hucke sat back in his chair. "I believe I can solve that," he said. "I have a friend who will help. He's a doctor. I will get in touch with him tomorrow." He opened a drawer in his desk, from which he took a small camera and passed it to her.

"This can be easily concealed. You can photograph documents, plans, whatever you find. Then take the reel of film to Eva. She will be able to pass it on to Otto. If we are successful in this, it may provide us with important information vital to the Allies.

Herr Hucke supplied the drugs as promised, saying it would be necessary to use the contents of two of the capsules to be sure of full sedation. Hildegard put the capsules safely into her handbag and decided to test them on herself before using them on Karl.

When she got back to the house, she hid the camera in a drawer amongst her underwear. Then one night she told Frieda that she felt tired and was going to retire early, and Frieda gave her hot milk to take up to the bedroom. She had sufficient knowledge about drugs to know that because she was not in the habit of consuming much alcohol and was of small stature as well, it would require less to sedate her than Herr Hucke had said, so she emptied the contents of just one of the capsules into her drink.

She awoke the next morning with a headache and feeling heavy-eyed, realising that she'd missed breakfast. *I suppose a hangover must feel like this,* she thought. At least she'd gained more confidence about administering the drugs to Karl.

Karl came home for several brief visits before he announced that another meeting would be held. This would be her opportunity to carry out the plan. Meanwhile, she endeavoured to remain calm and to behave as normal. On the day of the meeting, she wore a skirt with a side pocket, in which she placed two of the capsules. It was late when Karl joined her in the lounge upstairs after the meeting had ended.

"You look tired, my love," she said truthfully. "Sit there and I will pour you a drink." She hated what she was about to do, but there was no turning back.

"Only a small one, please," said Karl, stretching his legs and closing his eyes.

She went over to the side table. Her hands were shaking as she poured brandy into two of the glasses. After glancing in the mirror above the table to be sure that Karl was not watching her, she tipped the contents of the capsules into one of the glasses and handed it to him before sitting down again. She wondered how long it would take the drug to take effect and hoped he would not fall asleep where he was. He was still holding the glass when he'd finished the brandy. Seeing that he was becoming drowsy, she took the glass from his hand. This had the desired effect of waking him.

He yawned. "I am exhausted, darling," he said. "Would you mind if I retire to bed?"

"No," she assured him. "It's late. I'll come too."

He quickly fell asleep, and for about an hour, she lay listening to the sound of his breathing before deciding it would be safe to make her move. His keys were on the table by the bed. She pushed them into the pocket of her dressing gown along with the camera and a small torch.

She quietly crept down the stairs. When she reached Karl's study, she opened the door and put on the light, carefully pulling the door behind her but not completely closing it.

She held her breath when the door was slowly pushed open again a few moments later, but then breathed a sigh of relief when the dog flopped down beside her. There were many books in Karl's study, so if anyone came downstairs, she planned to say that she couldn't sleep and was looking for something to read.

Luckily, Karl's briefcase was unlocked, so she knew that any papers of importance would be in his desk. She finally found the correct key and discovered that the desk was double-locked. When eventually she was able to open the drawer, she found a variety of documents and plans and photographed all of them. This she did methodically, being careful to replace them exactly as she'd found them.

Afterwards, she locked the drawer and crept back upstairs.

It had taken her just over half an hour. When she climbed back into the bed, Karl was sleeping soundly. She lay beside him for a long time with her heart pounding before falling asleep herself.

He left for Berlin the next day, and Hildegard walked to the village after making an excuse to visit the drapery shop, where she passed the reel of film to Eva and received a new reel in return.

Over the following months, there were frequent meetings at the house, and on random occasions, she repeated the process of photographing the documents locked in Karl's desk. She had decided that it would be unwise to carry out the operation too often, as Karl might link the drinks she gave him with his excessive tiredness. Apart from that, Herr Hucke had told her that the information she obtained was being passed on to British intelligence; she was concerned that if the British acted on it every time a meeting took place, the Germans would one day suspect a leak. She had to prevent them from associating any leak with someone at the house.

After a while, the meetings became less frequent, but there was one occasion when she had made up her mind to repeat the process, had just finished photographing some plans, and was returning them to the drawer when she heard someone outside the study. There were some other documents left on the desk, but she managed to close the drawer and put the camera in her pocket as the door was opened. It was Schultz.

"What are you doing, Fräulein?" he asked in a demanding voice.

Having already decided to exercise her authority as the colonel's lady with anyone who challenged her, Hildegard spoke sharply.

"More to the point, Schultz, what are you doing coming into the colonel's study at night?"

"I thought I heard someone moving about down here, Fräulein," he said in a more subdued tone, no doubt realising that he may have spoken out of turn by questioning her.

"I was in the kitchen before I came in here for a book, and I heard nothing," she said. "I should be quite surprised if you could have heard me from upstairs, on the second floor of the house."

Schultz was clearly searching for an excuse. "I must have been mistaken. I'm sorry."

"I think the dog would have barked and warned us had a stranger been moving about," she said, glancing down at Wrex, who was lying quietly by the desk.

Schultz looked concerned. "Will you be telling the colonel?" he asked.

"I see no reason for that. You were right to be vigilant." She gave him a brief smile and hoped that she had handled the incident satisfactorily.

He looked relieved. "Thank you. Good night, Fräulein."

"Good night, Schultz. You can leave the door open. I'm going back to the kitchen again now."

Hildegard was sure that he could not have heard her moving about, for she'd been careful to make no noise. He must have come down for some other purpose and for this reason would be unlikely to tell anyone about the incident. *Perhaps it will serve as a mutual understanding between the two of us for the future*, she thought. She was not sure how much he had seen. He could not have known whether the papers which she had taken from Karl's briefcase and left on the desk were left there by Karl unless he had been in the room previously, which he would not want to reveal.

She believed that she had managed to slip the camera into her pocket before he could have noticed it.

After waiting a while, she listened at the bottom of the stairs until she was sure that Schultz had gone back up, and then she returned to the study, where she quickly finished photographing the remaining documents. After that, she went to the kitchen and made herself a mug of hot milk, deliberately leaving the mug and pan in evidence. To forestall Schultz, she would make a point of telling Frieda the next morning that she had been down to the kitchen to make a hot drink because she had been unable to sleep. When at last she returned to the bedroom, she checked that Karl was still sleeping soundly before returning the keys to the pocket of his uniform jacket where she had found them.

It was not until she was lying down again that she realised that she was wet with perspiration, and she decided that it would be too risky to carry out the exercise again for some time. The encounter with Schultz was certainly puzzling. Had it been his original intention to go into the study, and if so, for what reason? If not, what was he doing down there? The more she thought about it, the more she was certain that he could not have heard her moving about. Schultz remained a mystery.

For some reason, Karl was not returning to Berlin the following day as he usually did after a meeting. She had to go to the village to pass the reel of film to Eva and decided that the best time would be early in the morning, when Karl would be working in his study, and since it was a Saturday, she would probably take Elsa with her.

The next day was bright and sunny, and as soon as they finished breakfast, Hildegard and Elsa walked to the village. She left Elsa looking at some old books on a stand next door to the drapery shop and then went to speak to Eva.

"Have you any handkerchiefs like this?" she enquired, handing over her own handkerchief in which she had concealed the film.

It was always difficult to find the right time to pass the film to Eva so that the other woman serving in the shop did not become suspicious.

"Not like this, but how about these?" said Eva, putting a small box on the counter and leaning forward as she whispered, "I will see that it is passed on tonight."

Hildegard whispered back in reply, "Good—I cannot get any more for some time."

When they returned home, Hildegard saw that Karl had finished his work and was there to greet them. He told her that there would be no more meetings for a while, so he would be able to spend a little more time with her over the summer months. This was heaven-sent, and it meant that her problems would be solved for the time being, without the need to make any further excuses.

It was now June, and it had been nearly six months since Max had returned to active service, so when Karl said that he was coming on leave and they could expect a visit from him again in the near future, she was pleased.

She wondered, though, if it meant that his unit was being replaced, because she knew that things were not going well and that the German army was being pushed back on the Russian front.

As it was a warm, sunny day, Hildegard and Karl spent the afternoon in the garden together. She remembered the previous summer, which had been the happiest time of her life. It was almost a year since she had come to live with him. She could never think about the future and would never be able to reconcile her activities over the last few months with her love for him. Now at least she could forget all the difficulties for a while.

Karl had promised to take her out for dinner that evening. For the occasion, she put on a dress she hadn't worn before. She'd bought it when she and Lotta first went shopping. The dress was cut a little lower than she would have liked, but she wanted to wear something new and special for Karl because they so seldom had an opportunity to go out together. He had put on his uniform, and that always meant that they would receive preferential treatment in the restaurants.

"All the men will be looking at you in that dress, darling," he remarked when he saw her.

"And all the women will be looking at my handsome colonel and will envy me," she replied.

She thought then of her German mother. Had she lived and had there not been a war, how proud her mother would have been if she had married a man like Karl, who came from a grand old German family. As it was, she was never likely to marry the man she loved and have his children. Their time together would probably be brief, but time was relative. They were together now, and she was happy.

"You are suddenly very quiet—what are you thinking about?" he asked.

"Oh, nothing of importance," she said, looking up at him.

He smiled lovingly. "I feel I have neglected you of late when I have been here. I felt so tired last night that I must have fallen asleep before you came to bed."

"Please don't worry about it," she said. "I understand. I know you have been working hard."

As he bent to kiss the top of her head, she flinched. "Yes, yes, I know," he said, laughing and drawing back. "I must not spoil your hair!"

She smiled up at him. She was so thankful that it would not be necessary for her to use sedatives again for the time being, perhaps not for the whole summer. She would make every moment count.

The months ahead were indeed idyllic. Karl came home as often as he could, and she imagined how it might be if, by some miracle, they both survived the war. Naturally, there were things about which they might disagree; for one thing, she could never approve of the way Elsa was being raised. She led too sheltered a life and needed a chance to mix with other children. Karl liked to control and protect his own, and that included herself as well as Elsa. Although she understood his reasons for this in wartime, she couldn't help wondering if he would act in the same way if Germany were no longer at war. For now, of course, she was careful always to agree with whatever he said or suggested. *Perhaps that's the reason we're so happy together,* she thought.

Although there were no doubts in her mind that she loved him, doubts about other matters were ever present. She found herself thinking often about all the things she could never ask him. He was a good man, kind and considerate, always courteous to women and caring and protective of his family, so how could he be a Nazi? She felt sure that he was not a member of the party, but did he approve of the Fascist regime, and what was his attitude towards their treatment of the Jews? She remembered his apparent protection of Schultz, the gardener, whom she now felt sure was Jewish, or was this just another instance of his desire to protect whatever or whoever he regarded as one of his possessions? There were so many things to which she may never know the answers. But for now, life at the house went on the same, and she accepted it and was happy.

The time for Max's visit came, and Karl said he would be bringing an old girlfriend with him. Hildegard was looking forward to this. Although she had Frieda's friendship, she still missed the company of her women friends—but Karl told her that Max's girlfriends were not usually the sort of girls he would want to introduce to his mother.

"We shall provide them with two guest rooms," he told her, "and whether or not they occupy both rooms will be up to them."

"Perhaps they will do what we did and creep from room to room," she replied.

His answer was that it was different because they were in love. When he brought her to live at his house, it was as his wife in all but name. She realised that Karl was quite conventional after all.

Max and his girlfriend arrived that evening. The young woman, probably in her late twenties, was tall with a good figure and long brown hair. She wore a low-cut dress and occasionally puffed at a cigarette through a long holder held between her brightly painted lips. Her name was Jutta. She spent much of the evening teasing Max, something he actually seemed to enjoy. As the evening progressed, she even tried her tactic on Karl, but that didn't go down too well, so she quickly dropped it. Nevertheless, Hildegard enjoyed the evening because she liked Max and found it informative as well because she didn't often get a chance to see Karl's reactions to the presence of a stranger. Although he was always polite to Jutta, his manner was cool and he appeared disinterested. It was a side of him that she didn't really know, and it reminded her of his attitude towards Herr Hucke when Herr Hucke first introduced him to her. He clearly didn't approve of this particular girlfriend that Max had brought to the house.

"I'm sorry about Jutta," he said later when they were alone together. "She is not very good company for you, and I'm not sure that her presence creates a suitable atmosphere for Elsa. It is just as well that they're only here for a few days."

"If you'd like to spend some time with Max, I will try to entertain her," said Hildegard, "although I don't think she has taken to me."

"I think perhaps she sees you as a rival for centre stage, darling, even with Max. I cannot send them away, though. Max has little enough pleasure in his life, and if she pleases him, I think we have to try to accept her."

After breakfast the next morning, all of them, including Elsa, walked into the garden. A few moments later, the dog bounded out of the house and dashed up to Jutta to investigate the new visitor. At the sight of him, she screamed and shrank away. "I hate dogs!" she shouted. "Get him away from me!"

That was enough for Elsa. She ran back to the house to report the incident to Frau Becker, who took her into the village in the afternoon and obligingly kept her amused for the rest of Jutta's stay. Hildegard knew that Karl was fond of his cousin and that the visit must have been a disappointment to him.

Max was to come just one more time before going back on active service.

Chapter 7

A NEAR THING

As the Fräulein was coming from the kitchen after lunch, she stopped to chat to Hildegard, which was unusual; she even asked about her health. When the Fräulein had gone, Hildegard found herself laughing.

"What has happened to Ursula?" she asked. "She is unusually affable."

"Yes, I've just heard she has a boyfriend at last," said Frieda.

"Well, that is good news. I wonder what he's like."

"I think he's a friend of her brother Klaus."

"Is he in the SS too?" Hildegard enquired, hoping he was not.

"Yes, I think so," said Frieda. "Perhaps she will be a happier girl now. It might make Elsa's life better if she were."

"I wonder if we shall see him. Perhaps she'll bring him here. I shouldn't think she would want to go to Berlin. The colonel says there are air raids there almost every night."

Hildegard didn't know whether the Fräulein would be a less likely enemy now or not. Although she had told Karl about the Fräulein's brother being in the SS, he had said little in response.

She still had no idea what he thought about the SS. She knew that they were not always highly regarded by the Wehrmacht. They had been hardened and specially trained to be cruel. Of one thing, she was certain: she would need to be very careful of the Fräulein now, particularly if she prevailed upon Karl to let her brother or boyfriend spend his leave at the house. Hildegard knew that Frieda's young son, who was in the German navy and served on a U-boat, stayed at the house whenever he had leave. She reasoned, though, that as Ursula's parents were alive, her brother would surely stay with them. She just hoped it would be the same with her boyfriend. She didn't think Karl would allow soldiers to come to the house while Elsa was around, and they might become suspicious of Schultz as well.

Hildegard had gone to report to Herr Hucke, and after a brief session with him, Lotta appeared and announced that there was a job for Hildegard. It seemed that one of the group's contacts at the university in Heidelberg needed someone to translate documents from English to German. It was sensitive material; it couldn't be handed to an official translator without revealing the name of the person doing the work. Herr Hucke had suggested Hildegard. The contact had agreed, and Hildegard was pleased to help. Lotta said that she knew Heidelberg well and would accompany her, being friendly with an elderly couple who owned a café near the university, with whom they would be able to stay for a few days.

The contact was a physicist named Dr Muller. He had told Herr Hucke that they only needed to be in Heidelberg for a few days. The job would not take long but Hildegard would have to attend the university each day because the documents she would be translating couldn't be taken away.

She was looking forward to working as a translator at last. The elderly couple had provided them with comfortable rooms, and they would be able to eat their meals at the café. On the first day of Hildegard's assignment, Lotta accompanied her to the university to introduce her to Dr Muller. The papers she was to work on were technical, and she didn't understand them. But she was pleased when she found that the actual passages for translation were quite straightforward. Therefore, the job seemed to be going well—that is, until the second day of their stay.

They were in the café at lunchtime and both noticed a man sitting at a nearby table. He had been there at lunch the day before and seemed to be watching them. Lotta told her that he'd left the café at the same time they did. She said that she had already decided to visit a museum that afternoon while Hildegard was working. Since the route took them past the university, they would be able to walk part of the way together. Then, if the man followed them out of the café again, she would be able to see which one of them he was following. When they got up to go, Hildegard saw the man get up too. Again he left the café when they left.

"Perhaps he works at the university and it is just a coincidence that he leaves at the same time we do," she said, not wanting to show her concern, even to Lotta.

"This is possible," said Lotta, "but we must be careful. There are several possibilities. He may be interested in Dr Muller and hoping to get at him in some way through you, or he may be following me for some reason. Another possibility is that Colonel von Richter has become suspicious of you and is having you watched."

"He's shown no signs of suspecting me so far," said Hildegard. She was thinking that if he was having her watched, it was just as likely to be for her protection.

To discuss the situation, the two women met up again that evening at a restaurant about half a kilometre from the café where they were staying.

"The man turned down a street opposite the entrance to the university," said Lotta, "and after that I became convinced that it was, after all, just a coincidence that he'd been in the café the day before. But then, as I was leaving the museum, I saw him again. I could tell he knew I'd seen him. He knows, of course, that we are together and staying at the café. I shall come with you to the university tomorrow to see Dr Muller and tell him of our concern. He will be able to make radio contact with Herr Hucke, who will know what's best for us to do."

Two days later, before she left, Dr Muller told Hildegard that the job was completed. He said also that he had heard from Herr Hucke, who said that she and Lotta should stay on at the café for an additional two days and behave as normal. He was sending Otto to take care of the problem.

Lotta seemed relieved when she heard what Dr Muller had said. "We can look round the city tomorrow," she said. "I'll take you to the museum, and there are many other places of interest we can visit."

Hildegard was becoming more concerned that Karl might be having her watched after all. She didn't want to express her concern to Lotta, because she would never understand that he might be doing so for her protection and not because he suspected she was a spy.

"We will return to the café for lunch tomorrow," said Lotta, "and follow the same routine."

There was, however, one variation the next day. They were in the middle of lunch when the man they suspected of following them entered the café with another man; they joined a third man sitting on the other side of the café.

After a while, the three men stood up and went to the table near the one where they had been sitting. Hildegard heard one of them say, "Your papers, please."

They moved from table to table until they came to Hildegard and Lotta's table.

"This is a routine check, ladies. We need to see your papers."

"You're an interpreter and translator, Fräulein," said one of the men. "Are you working at the university?"

"Yes," said Hildegard, "but the job is finished now. I only had five days of work." Her hands were clammy. She felt sure there were beads of perspiration on her forehead, but she tried to behave as though she were untroubled by their questions.

"How did you come to be given a job there?" asked the other man.

"I wrote to the university," she said, "and was told that if I came here, there might be work for me." She felt her heart beating rapidly.

The man took some time before returning their documents. "Thank you, ladies," he said and they passed on to the next table.

"I'll come to your room with you." Lotta smiled as she picked up her bag and coat when they had finished their meal.

"What do you make of that?" asked Hildegard as soon as they were in her room together.

"Well, I personally think their interest is in Dr Muller and that it was a mistake for us to have come here. Perhaps, though, they will lose interest in us now that they know you will have no further contact with him."

They saw nothing of the man from the café during the following daytime, but when they were having a meal there in the evening, he was back again. This time, he spoke to them.

"Good evening, ladies. Have you had a good day?"

"I took my niece to the market," chirped Lotta, "and then this afternoon we went to the museum. We are both going home tomorrow."

"Have you enjoyed your brief stay here, Fräulein?" he asked, turning to Hildegard.

"Yes, I like Heidelberg very much."

"Do you often work as a translator and interpreter?"

The two men who had examined their papers had clearly briefed him.

"Not really. I'm a friend of Colonel von Richter, and I tutor his daughter in English and French. That's the reason I should return now."

The man smiled. "Do you live at his home?" he asked.

"Yes," she said simply.

"You are very pretty, Fräulein, a flower of Germany and a credit to our country."

"Thank you." Hildegard concluded that he thought she was the colonel's plaything whenever he returned home from his duties. The man left the café soon afterwards, and they were able to finish their meal in peace.

"I think that passed off all right, don't you?" asked Hildegard.

"One thing we know for sure now is that he's Gestapo," said Lotta. "It is well that you are a blue-eyed blonde, Hildegard. These Nazis are obsessed with the idea of the pure Aryan race, and they think the role of such women is to please men and to have children."

After breakfast the next morning, Lotta went out alone for a short walk. She returned with a newspaper which she took to Hildegard's room and sat scanning through it.

"Yes!" Lotta called out suddenly. "Come and look at this!" She pointed to a small paragraph on an inside page:

> *The bodies of two men were found near the university in Heidelberg last night. One of the men had been shot and the other appeared to have been strangled. Both men are believed to have been members of the security forces. An arrest is imminent.*

Hildegard felt the blood drain from her face. The reality of her involvement with the German Resistance was coming closer.

"Three men came here," said Lotta. "Otto has obviously taken care of two of them, but we don't know what has happened to the third, so I think we must leave right away. We will pack your things in my case and get rid of your smaller one. That way, you will look less like a traveller. Gestapo could be watching the station here for suspects, so I think we should split up and meet at the next station out of Heidelberg. We should go by bus. I will show you where to catch the bus and then take a slightly different route myself. You may arrive at the station before I do, but you can wait for me in the waiting room. The sooner we get away from here, the better."

As she sat waiting for Lotta, Hildegard couldn't help wondering again if there was any possibility that Karl had her watched or even whether it could have anything to do with the Fräulein. Perhaps one of the men was Klaus, Ursula Fischer's brother, yet that was unlikely because no one at the house knew that she and Lotta had gone to Heidelberg.

When Lotta arrived, they checked the times of the trains, and Hildegard went back with her. Hildegard was planning to return home to the colonel's house the following day. Herr Hucke had been anxious and was glad to see them back. He said that unfortunately, Otto had lost track of the third man and was still uncertain which of them he was. Lotta was sure that the man who had followed them was Gestapo, while the other two were SS, and according to the paragraph in the newspaper, the men found dead were SS. Lotta told Herr Hucke of their conversation with the man who had followed them from the café, adding that Hildegard had told him that she lived at the colonel's house. Hildegard was concerned in case she had said too much. She was pleased when Herr Hucke said that he saw no problem in what she had said.

Hildegard returned home and was met by Frieda, who said that the colonel was back. She at once became apprehensive. Was this to be the showdown, the recriminations, the punishment, or even worse, the arrest? After a few moments of concern, she grew calm. She was being ridiculous. If Karl suspected her of being a spy, she would either have been arrested by now or he would have challenged her and demanded an explanation. Instead, he came into the room smiling as he approached her, but then, when he raised his hand to tilt her head and kiss her, she flinched. It was an involuntary reaction. For just one second, she'd thought he might be going to hit her.

When he saw her reaction, he drew back. "What's wrong, Hildegard?" he enquired anxiously.

She immediately put her arms round him. "I'm sorry, Karl. I don't know what's the matter with me. I have such a headache. It must be because the train was crowded and I had to stand for much of the journey home. I went to see my aunt, and we went to Heidelberg for a few days because I had a job there. It's all been rather tiring."

Hildegard had thought it best to tell him all this right away in order to see his response. She didn't want it to be drawn out. She needn't have worried.

"You must lie down for a while, darling," he said. "I'll send Frieda to give you something for your headache."

Frieda came into the room with an aspirin, a glass of warm milk, and a cold sponge to put on her forehead. She spoke reassuringly: "Try to get some sleep and you'll soon feel better."

None of this was what Hildegard wanted. Whenever Karl came home, it was a honeymoon for them. She looked forward to his brief visits so much, despite the meetings that he often held at the house and the ensuing ritual.

An hour later, she got up, combed her hair, powdered her face, and went in search of Karl. She found him in his study. He looked up and smiled when she entered the room. "Are you feeling better now?"

She smiled back at him. "I am quite all right now, Karl."

"Good. Frieda is preparing dinner now, but we will go out somewhere special for dinner tomorrow. I have two further days of leave, and we can spend most of the time together. You should have an early night."

"It isn't necessary. There's nothing wrong with me now."

He was smiling. "Good," he repeated. "Then let's both have an early night tonight."

By the end of Karl's leave, she was confident that he'd had no hand in what happened in Heidelberg. After he left, her attention turned to the Fräulein.

As Hildegard always felt low after Karl had gone, she usually went to talk to Frieda. They sometimes spent the evenings together, especially if Frieda's husband was out. Herr Becker often visited a friend who was crippled due to an injury he sustained in an air raid while working in Berlin.

When Elsa went to bed, the Fräulein liked to go to her room and read, whereas Herr Becker and Frieda would retire to their sitting room. On this occasion, though, Herr Becker went out, so Hildegard invited Frieda to spend the evening with her. Frieda came in with coffee, and Hildegard raided Karl's wine cabinet for a small tot of brandy for each. After a while, she managed to steer the conversation round to the Fräulein.

"How's Ursula's romance progressing?" she asked.

"I don't think it's going too well at the moment. I can usually tell because she takes it out on Elsa, who sometimes comes to me in tears." "Oh, poor child", Hildegard said, shaking her head.

"Do you know if her brother is still in Berlin?"

"Yes, I think so. I hear more about him than about the boyfriend these days."

"They're both in the SS, aren't they?"

"So she says."

"Karl would be concerned if he thought she was upsetting Elsa."

Frieda nodded. "I don't want to worry the colonel unnecessarily, but if it continues, I think I shall have to tell him about it next time he is here."

"Meanwhile," said Hildegard, "I'll see if I can get her to talk to me about her boyfriend. I would have thought she'd have been as keen to tell me about him as she was to tell me about her brother, who she said met the Führer. I'll let you know if I'm successful."

"I wish you luck," Frieda said with a smile.

Herr Becker returned a moment later, and Frieda left to join him. Hildegard planned how to approach Ursula Fischer to talk as much as possible about both her brother and her boyfriend. She already knew that Ursula was proud that her brother was in the SS. She felt sure that she must have a photograph of him. Hildegard was still concerned about Ursula's connection with members of the SS, but she felt it only a remote possibility that the Fräulein could have persuaded her brother to have her followed when away from the house. However, she had shown jealousy over Karl, and if she'd lost her boyfriend, it might have rekindled that jealousy.

Although the Fräulein could not have known in advance that she would be going to Heidelberg, any more than she'd known it herself, there was a possibility that someone could have followed her there. Hildegard thought that if she could get the Fräulein to show her a photograph of her brother, she might be able to eliminate him as being one of the men who came to the café. Of course, she was particularly concerned about the third man, who had escaped Otto's attention. The man whom Olga had said was Gestapo was definitely too old to be either the Fräulein's brother or her boyfriend. If her brother had been killed, she would know by now, Hildegard reasoned. So her boyfriend should be the main subject of her investigation.

She needed to create an opportunity to talk to the Fräulein. Then she got an idea. As she wanted to visit the nearby town to look for a small gift for Karl for his birthday, Hildegard asked Frieda if she thought Herr Becker would have time one day to drive her there. She wanted to take Elsa along too—and the Fräulein as well, if she would like to accompany them.

The outing was duly arranged, and as she was always anxious that her role not be usurped, the Fräulein was pleased to join them on the excursion. On the appointed day, they all had an early breakfast and Herr Becker drove them to the nearby town and agreed to pick them up again in the afternoon. They visited various shops, and the Fräulein and Elsa made some small purchases. Hildegard hadn't yet been able to find the book she wanted for Karl, so she took them to a restaurant for lunch and planned for them to visit another bookshop and the department store afterwards.

When they were seated in the restaurant, Hildegard was able to steer the conversation to the Fräulein's brother. "My brother has been promoted," the Fräulein volunteered. "We're all very proud of him, and he's just become engaged to a girl from Hamburg, where our parents live."

"Do your brother and boyfriend serve together?" Hildegard enquired.

"They used to," said the Fräulein, "but Boris, my boyfriend, has been sent away on special duties. I haven't heard from him for some time, and I cannot write to him because I don't know where he is."

"I shouldn't worry, Ursula," Hildegard said. "If he is on special duties, he may not be allowed to contact you. Perhaps your brother will be able to get in touch with him. Your brother's name is Klaus, isn't it? When is Klaus to be married?"

"I don't really know. They'll probably wait for his next leave."

"Well, don't forget—I shall want to see the wedding photographs."

The Fräulein looked pleased and dived into her handbag. "This is a photograph of Klaus and Boris together," she said.

"They are both good-looking young men, aren't they?"

said Hildegard.

To Hildegard's relief, they were not the men she had seen at the café in Heidelberg. She was sure now that the episode in Heidelberg had no connection with Karl or anyone at the house, which meant that the man who Lotta believed to be Gestapo was probably more interested in Dr Muller than in Lotta or herself.

She let a few days elapse before visiting Lotta and Herr Hucke to report her findings. Herr Hucke said that it confirmed his own conclusion. He explained that Dr Muller was one of several scientists involved in the development of a new type of bomb that would become a flying bomb, more like an unmanned aeroplane. The military were placing great store on this new weapon and going to great pains to ensure that no information about it was leaked to the Allies. Dr Muller was now aware that he was under suspicion, and the Resistance were planning his escape.

When Hildegard returned home the following day, there was further news from Frieda.

"Our little Elsa's life should improve now," Frieda said. "Ursula has at last heard from her boyfriend, and she thinks that he may get a few days of leave when her brother gets married."

"I'm glad it won't be necessary to burden the colonel with our problems here."

Frieda nodded. "I agree. It would be a pity if it became necessary to replace the Fräulein, because I think she is a good teacher despite her moods. She must not be allowed to upset Elsa, but perhaps it will not happen again."

Hildegard planned to go to the nearby town once more because she was still looking for a gift for Karl. But this time she would go there alone. There had not been much time to look for a present for him when they all went together. They had spent too long over lunch and then on shopping for classroom essentials for Elsa and a new holdall for the Fräulein. A bus ran from the station in the village, and she thought it would be best to go early in the morning. She could walk into the village if necessary and take a taxi home from the station on her return. She'd done it once or twice before.

The town was about twenty kilometres away, and the journey from the village was a pleasant one. It was not a big town, but there were several small bookshops with both new and second-hand books for sale. She wanted a book about miniature paintings because she knew that nothing would please Karl more. There were a few books on art at the first shop she visited, but the second one looked more promising. It had a separate art section, and she spent some time looking through all the books on the shelves before finding what she wanted. It was as she turned to take the book to the assistant at the counter by the door that she realised a man was watching her. She hesitated and pretended to re-examine one of the other books on the shelf as though she were undecided. Then she picked up the first book again. As she turned once more to go to the counter, she looked across to where the man was standing and saw that he was still looking at her. This time, he smiled. He was not wearing a uniform, and she doubted he was much older than herself. He didn't look like Gestapo, but the episode in Heidelberg had made her nervous and suspicious of anyone who appeared to be watching her. She realised that he was coming over to speak to her.

He had a couple of books in his hand. "It looks as though you have been lucky too," he said. "I've been searching for one of these books for a long time, and at last I've found a second-hand copy."

She was taken by surprise because she had half expected him to say he was Gestapo and ask to see her identity papers. It didn't occur to her that a young man might be watching her because he liked the look of her.

She smiled at him. "Yes, the book I've chosen is a present for someone, and it's just what I wanted."

"There is a small bar just opposite. Would you like to go for a drink of some sort and then we could talk about our lucky finds?"

"Thank you," she said, "but I should be making my way back to the station. My bus runs from there and is due to leave on the hour."

"I could give you a lift to the station if you like." "No, I prefer to walk," said Hildegard, edging away. "Sorry, I cannot offer to walk with you. It's because of this . . ." He tapped his leg.

She hadn't noticed until then that he was carrying a walking stick. "Oh, I'm sorry. I didn't realise... Have you been injured?"

"I lost my leg fighting on the Russian front. I was a captain in the army, but I'm out of it now. It's not so bad, though. It's surprising what you learn to do with an artificial leg. I can even drive a car. There are many worse off than me."

Hildegard felt sorry for him and regretted not being friendlier. "I think I would like that drink after all," she said. "I would probably be too late now for the bus I'd planned to catch, but the one which leaves an hour later will do just as well."

The young man looked pleased. "I'm Ernst," he said a few moments later as they made their way to the bar, "and you are...?"

"I'm Hildegard."

"So you don't live in the town?"

"No, I live in a village twenty kilometres away, and you?"

"I live just the other side of the town. My father is the local doctor here. One of these books I've bought is for him. I owe such a lot to him. He has taught me how to overcome my handicap and tells me that if I can learn to ignore it, so will other people."

"He sounds like a wise man."

Perhaps I should apply some of that philosophy to myself, she thought. *Instead of becoming nervous whenever I see anyone watching me, I should learn to look as though I am enjoying it and expect it. In doing that, I would be less likely to arouse suspicion.*

The young man broke into her thoughts. "Have you a boyfriend?"

"Yes, I am with someone," she said. "The book is a gift for him."

"Lucky man. Is he in the army?"

"Yes, he fought in the desert campaign, and he too was wounded. He's been declared unfit for active service for a while."

"But he isn't out of it like me?"

"No. He's in the regular army, you see. The army is his career."

"He's a commissioned officer in the Wehrmacht, then."

The young man laughed. "If I'm not careful, I might be accused of trying to steal his girlfriend."

"You couldn't do that. No one could. But I am sure you have a girlfriend, Ernst."

"I did have, but she didn't wait for me. When I came back home, I found she'd married a naval man. Third officer on a U-boat, I think he is."

"I'm sorry."

"Oh, don't be. It happens in times like these."

"With your charm and positive attitude towards life, Ernst, I am sure you will achieve great things."

They talked about books and his ambition to teach until she had finished her coffee and he'd drained his beer.

"I should be going now," she said. "I have enjoyed our chat very much."

The young man smiled. "I think I'll stay for a while longer and have another beer."

Impulsively she bent and kissed his cheek.

"Your soldier is a lucky man to have someone like you, Hildegard," the young man said.

That's far from so, she thought, but she smiled.

"Goodbye. I hope your father likes the book."

When at last Hildegard arrived back home, she was pleased that she had gone alone and felt that she had learned a valuable lesson. Later she parcelled up the book she'd bought for Karl so that she could post it in the village next day. She had also bought two leather bookmarks to show to Elsa because she thought she might like to choose one to send to him; they could then post the items at the same time.

Although she no longer thought the Gestapo or anyone at the house knew she was a spy, Hildegard couldn't get the events of the last few weeks out of her mind. She'd been brought close to the reality of what might happen if she was found out. She wondered what had become of Dr Muller. One of the three men at the café had survived, most likely the Gestapo man, according to Lotta and Herr Hucke. Would Otto escape detection, or would his actions lead them to other members of the group? It had made her realise how much the members of the Resistance depended on each other for their lives. Could they make her tell them about the other members of the group if the Gestapo arrested her? Perhaps she should keep her suicide tablets on her person when she was not at the house. Yet the tablets themselves could give her away if she were searched. She must remember to talk to Lotta about this, although Lotta didn't know about her intimate relationship with Karl von Richter—unless she had guessed by now.

Chapter 8

VISIONS OF FAMILY

One day towards the end of summer, Hildegard suddenly began to feel ill. She had gone down to breakfast, which usually consisted of coffee and rolls, when she fainted. Frieda had to help her back upstairs. She was very sick, so Frieda called for the doctor, who said she had a fever. He was not sure what was wrong, although it could be food poisoning, so she spent the day in bed.

That same night, she awakened around midnight and was surprised to see Karl sprawled on the sofa in their room, still wearing his uniform. He stirred when she spoke to him and came over to sit on the bed.

"Karl, what are you doing here?" she asked, but she guessed that Frieda must have contacted him. "I feel better now; you should get some rest."

"I wanted to make sure there is nothing seriously wrong. I'm glad that you're feeling better now. I have to go again early in the morning." He took her hand. "Although it is nothing we should plan for, darling, if you turned out to be pregnant anytime, I want you to know that I would be delighted."

"I'm not pregnant, my love," she said, surprised, and her eyes filled with tears because she knew how much he would have liked a son, something that was never likely to happen.

Karl left early the next morning, and later the doctor called and pronounced her fit enough to get up. She spent much of the day relaxing and thinking about what Karl had said, almost wishing that she had been pregnant.

Karl had promised to come back soon and take her away to the mountains for a few days. He kept his promise. They returned home on the last day of his brief leave, and as they had done on so many summer afternoons before, they sat on the seat near the stream at the bottom of the garden. On this occasion, though, they dared to dream of their future together when the war ended.

"You are still young, Hilda," said Karl. "We shall have plenty of time to make plans."

She knew that her recent indisposition had made him think about their having a child together. For once, she indulged in the same dream, but neither of them voiced their dreams. She didn't want to think about the impossibility of it; she just wanted Karl to be happy.

"I wish you could stay longer," she said, "but I know we are lucky to be able to spend as much time as we do together."

"For us, it is the present that counts, and we're happy now, aren't we?" asked Karl, as he put his arm around her shoulders.

"I'm always happy when you're here," she said truthfully, dreading the time when it all ended yet always hoping for a miracle because she couldn't live without hope.

During Karl's next visit, something happened which caused Hildegard to rethink her future and her allegiance. They had gone for a walk through the woods, taking Elsa with them, and as they came to fields which led to the village, they heard what sounded like a plane in trouble. The engine appeared to stall and then restart, and the plane had dropped very low. They could see that it was a British plane. It looked as though it was about to crash-land. A few moments later, there was an enormous thud, so they ran to the next field, where it had nose-dived into the ground. Karl told Elsa and Hildegard to stay well clear, as it could burst into flames at any moment; he then went over to the wreckage and pulled the pilot clear, dragging him a safe distance away. The pilot was alive but unconscious.

Hildegard went to look at him. He looked little more than a boy. "I think his leg might be broken," she said.

The young man appeared to be regaining consciousness, and Karl quickly searched him to check that he had no weapon.

"Are you in pain?" she enquired, speaking to him in English.

"My back..." he moaned.

"Don't try to move," she said, thinking he might have fractured his spine.

"Will you stay with him whilst I take Elsa back to the house and get medical help?" Karl asked.

"Yes, of course. What will they do with him?"

"He'll be taken to a military hospital until he is well enough to be sent to a prison camp." Elsa had been looking on in silence. He took her by the hand. "I'll be back soon" he called to Hildegard. "Don't go near the wreckage."

When they had gone, she knelt down beside the pilot to reassure him and let him know help was coming.

By now, he had regained consciousness. He spoke faintly: "Where am I?"

"You are in Germany. Your plane came down."

He became anxious as he began to remember what had happened. "But you speak English—are you English?"

"I'm German, but I've been to England and know parts of it very well," she said, continuing to talk to him to keep him awake so that he didn't slip back into unconsciousness.

Karl returned and suggested she go back to the house, but she told him she would prefer to stay until assistance arrived and then they could walk back together. It was on her conscience that she could give no real words of comfort to the young Englishman, and she felt she should remain on hand to interpret, if necessary, when medical help finally came.

When the young man had been taken away, and they'd returned home Hildegard asked Karl if she could visit the pilot at the military hospital before he was sent to the prison camp; she would like to show him that Germans were human and not the monsters he might have been led to believe by enemy propaganda. She was pleased when Karl agreed, especially when he said he knew the commandant in charge of the hospital and would contact him.

As Karl had only two days left before he was to return to Berlin, he arranged the visit for the next day. This meant that he could take her to the hospital, which was in a small town about an hour's drive away. When they arrived, they were met by the commandant, who was a short dapper man, apparently a doctor himself. He greeted Karl enthusiastically. She could see that they were old friends. After a while, all three went to the ward where the pilot was held, and the commandant called an orderly to take her to the young man's bedside, telling her that they would be back for her in five minutes. Then the commandant and Karl left the ward together.

Hildegard was not to be allowed to stay long. She could see why visitors would not be welcome, because when she looked around, she saw some pitiful sights. Some men were moaning, and some were probably dying. She noticed an armed guard posted at the end of the ward and wondered why it was necessary, as none of the patients looked as though they were capable of going anywhere, let alone escaping. Only two of them were out of bed—one was on crutches, and the other was in a wheelchair, appearing to have had his foot amputated. She sat down at the pilot's bedside, where the orderly had placed a chair for her. The young man looked surprised but smiled in recognition when she enquired if he remembered her.

"I was present when your plane came down and you were dragged from the wreckage," she said.

"Yes, I remember, and someone must have pulled me from the plane before it burst into flames."

"That's right. It was the man who came into the ward with me who pulled you to safety."

He looked puzzled. "I don't remember seeing an army colonel there."

"You were only semi-conscious at the time," she said, "and besides, he was not in uniform then."

"I probably owe my life to him."

"Well, I think you were lucky we were nearby because I think you would have burned alive had the colonel not pulled you clear."

"It was a brave thing to do. Please thank him for me." "I'll tell him what you said," she promised.

"You sound English," said the young man, not remembering their conversation when they were in the field awaiting medical help. "Are you English?"

"No, I'm German" she told him again, "but I'm an interpreter and speak several languages. I came to see how you were, and I understand that despite a broken leg and a fractured hip, you should make a complete recovery. I see you also hurt your wrist. When it's healed, you'll be able to write a letter home and send it through the Red Cross."

Noticing that Karl and the commandant had returned already, Hildegard wished the young man a speedy recovery and went to join them, thankful to get away from the ward. She was glad she'd seen the Englishman, though, because he'd reminded her of Philip, the young pilot she'd married at the beginning of the war. So much had happened since then; it seemed years ago now. She wondered if, as with this young man, Philip's plane had nose-dived to the ground. If so, she hoped he'd been killed instantly and hadn't suffered. She hated to think of him dying friendless in a ward such as the one she'd just visited.

The commandant insisted that he would provide lunch for them and during the meal mentioned that he'd heard Karl had been wounded too. So Karl explained how he'd been involved in the desert campaign and wounded on two occasions before being pronounced unfit for active service.

"I'm in intelligence now and based in Berlin," he said. "That's good," remarked the commandant.

"Yes, in some ways it is," Karl said. "I get generous leave, which pleases Hildegard, but I feel I should be on active service again because I think I'm fit enough now."

"You must let your doctors be the judge of that," said the commandant wisely, and Hildegard was pleased to hear him say it.

A guard entered the room and the commandant was called away, so Karl made an excuse for them to leave at the same time.

"I'm glad to get away," Hildegard said. "It was harrowing being in the ward where they had put him."

"A military hospital is never a pleasant place, my dear, but I understand that you wanted to know that the young man we rescued would recover from his injuries. It's always good when we can save a life rather than have to take a life, even if he is the enemy."

It was then that she realised she hadn't been thinking of this young pilot as her countryman but, as Karl had said, as the enemy. She had wanted to be sure that he would recover, but that was out of humanity. If the pilot had been German or French, he would still have reminded her of Philip. Her interest had not so much to do with his nationality as with what had happened to him when his plane came down in a foreign land far away from home. She hated all the suffering and misery.

"You must have seen some terrible things, Karl, when you were serving under Rommel."

"Yes, I've seen many men die—on both sides."

"I suppose there must have been times when you had to do things you would rather not have done. Did you worry about it?"

"I'm a professional soldier, Hilda. It is not for me to decide the course the war should take or to make decisions about what's right or wrong. It is my job to follow orders and to fight for my country, and that is what I do."

She wished she could have led the conversation on to ask him what he thought about the Nazi Party and the Jewish situation but knew she dare not take it any further. Karl did what all soldiers must do, whatever their nationalities. They fight for their countries, right or wrong. Many may not even question the ethics of what they do, but all the time she was with Karl, she felt that he had reservations about the way Germany was being led. However, she'd long ago resigned herself to never knowing for sure.

After the incident with the pilot, and when Karl had returned to Berlin, she began to examine her attitude to her own compatriots as opposed to the people she'd come to love in Germany. Those around her in her small world seemed so far removed from the evil regime that led them. She had come to accept these people as her own. Karl, Elsa, and Max were her family now. She no longer had anyone left in England. Her father would almost certainly have died from his illness, and her friends would probably have forgotten her. Even if they hadn't, they would be unlikely to want her friendship now that she lived with a German colonel—and not with any reluctance either.

Hildegard kept turning these things over in her mind and felt that her loyalty must surely be to those she loved, to her family here. Yet was it? She believed that Britain's war with Germany was a just war. One day she might be forced to choose between those she loved and her principles. It would be a terrible choice. *I am not a traitor, she thought. I risk my life. I pass information to the Resistance group to be relayed to British intelligence. I am doing the job I was sent to do, even though I hate what I am doing at times. Perhaps if I survive the war, one day I will make my life in Switzerland, a neutral country.* She found comfort in that thought.

She'd been sitting on the seat by the stream, where she and Karl loved to sit together. Now she got up and walked slowly up the path to the house. As she came near, Wrex ran up to greet her, and Elsa was close behind. She smiled and patted the dog. Elsa took her hand.

"Come on," she said, "let's go and see if Frieda has made some apple strudel for us."

"Oh, yes," said Elsa with delight. "Wrex seems to like cake too. He recognises the word. Look at his tail wagging."

Living here, Elsa was hardly aware of the war, she thought. Her father was a regular army man and had always been away from home a lot. She didn't mix with the children from families who might have suffered from the effects of the war, for Karl protected her from any such unpleasantness.

As the memory of the plane crash and the visit to the prison hospital faded, Hildegard felt happier and settled once more into the routine at the house. She was spending more time with Elsa and giving her extra tuition in English and French, as she had promised. Karl had not questioned her about her supposed job as an interpreter, but she planned to go away somewhere for a day or two just to keep the myth alive. As she had not had anything to report to Herr Hucke, it had been some months since she'd contacted Lotta. When she did, Lotta suggested they go to Switzerland together to visit her sister again. Hildegard could then return via Berlin. So on the way back, as in the past, Hildegard contacted Karl on her arrival and then took a taxi to Karl's headquarters.

When she entered the building, she reported to the official in charge, who arranged for a guard to escort her to Karl's office, and as she left with the man, she heard someone enquire who she was.

"That's the colonel's woman," said a man in uniform. There was loud laughter, and unfortunately for the soldier concerned, Karl, who had been on his way to meet her, overheard the remark. She had never seen him so angry. He took her back to his office and asked for the man to be sent to see him. When the soldier came, Karl threatened him with demotion if he was ever disrespectful again, also making him apologise to her.

Afterwards, she sat patiently waiting for Karl to finish his work so that they could go to her hotel, where they would dine and spend the rest of the evening together. *He looks so tired,* she thought, *and becomes angry more easily these days.* She felt that he was worried about the future and was sure that he no longer believed Germany could win the war.

At the hotel that evening, they sat at the same table in the restaurant where they had sat nearly eighteen months earlier, when Karl had asked her to accompany him to his home to meet Elsa and to stay for the few days of his leave.

Karl was looking at her gravely, and she could see that he was concerned.

"Hilda, my darling" he said, "should I not survive the war, I have provided for our house to be held in trust during the lifetime of any present member of my family. When my aunt dies, the old family home will be sold; the proceeds will be held in trust for the maintenance and upkeep of the house where we now live. I want you to know that although my aunt would become Elsa's guardian, I would want you to remain at the house if you wished to do so, and Elsa would be able to choose whether she wanted to stay at the house with you or go to live with her aunt."

"Karl, my love" she said anxiously, "are you expecting to be ordered back on active service?"

"I'm not sure, my darling, but I think I'm probably medically fit by now."

He still did not discuss with her the progress of the war, but she remembered the conversation she had overheard him having with Max.

The next day when she went back home, Elsa came running to meet her and hug her, just as she did her father.

The following few weeks passed quietly. By now, it was early December, and Karl took a few more days of leave, during which they had another visit from Max. He came alone this time. They talked and laughed once more and Karl entertained them at the piano. Despite the façade of cheerfulness, from the look on their faces, Hildagard suspected that they were all aware of the underlying tension but none of them discussed it. She was sad when the time came for Max to go. She and Karl arose early to see him off and wish him well. It was a cold winter's morning, and an icy wind was blowing when Herr Becker brought the car round to the front of the house in order to drive Max to the station. Before getting into the car, he waved at them and smiled, shouting goodbye. She did not know it then, but it was the last time they would all be together.

The month of December passed, and Karl had managed only two days of leave at Christmas. It was too quiet at the house, and she felt cut off from what was happening.

Chapter 9

A SHOCK AWAKENING

Karl had not managed to come home for some time, and Hildegard was missing him. She decided to visit Lotta because it was time that she reported to Herr Hucke. Afterwards, she would catch a train through to Berlin instead of returning home. She planned to tell Karl that she had helped out as an interpreter in an emergency and so had returned via Berlin. She knew he wouldn't question this, and as soon as she arrived, she telephoned him as usual and was surprised to learn that he would be able to travel back with her. It would mean that her subterfuge was unnecessary, but she was delighted that he would be coming home. They agreed that Hildegard would take a taxi to his office and wait for him there. On discovering that there were no taxis available, she decided to make the short journey on foot. As she had only travelled to Karl's office by car, she was shocked to see the amount of bomb damage. Berlin was a city in ruins.

When she finally arrived at the square where Karl's office was located, she found that a huge crowd had gathered and thought it must be some sort of rally. A man was addressing the cheering and shouting crowd. Then there was a sudden disturbance near where she was standing. Men who Hildegard supposed were Gestapo were directing SS security forces, who were dragging two men away and bundling them into a van. One of the captives was an old man, and the other was much younger. While this was happening, the man addressing the crowd engaged in anti-semetic abuse and the crowd shouted in response, "Jude!, Jude". Soon they were singing patriotic songs, and they broke into "Deutschland Über Alles". Hildegard had once loved the stirring sound of the German anthem, but now, as she stood there in the square, her blood ran cold. How could these people, the same people with whom she had lived as a child, be so blindly led and so filled with hatred? If she had doubts before, she no longer had any left now. The job that she had been sent to do far outweighed her own personal feelings in importance. She and Karl were casualties of war, and she had to accept that.

The jeering and shouting crowd had become even louder as they sang their patriotic songs. As she watched, she remembered a play called *The Mob*, by John Galsworthy, which her class had studied in her final year at school. One particular passage she'd had to learn by heart came into her mind. *It could never be more relevant than now,* she thought as she recited it to herself:

You—Mob—are the most contemptible thing
under the sun.
When you walk the street—God goes in...
You are the thing that pelts the weak;

Kicks women; howls down free speech.
This today, and that tomorrow.
Brain—you have none.
Spirit—not the host of it!

For some time, Hildegard continued to stand there, lost in her thoughts, until she noticed a young woman cowering in a doorway. She guessed she was probably trying to hide from the SS, who had dragged the men away. She wished she could do something to help her, but she didn't know what. Noticing that the SS men were coming back, Hildegard turned away and ran up the steps to the building that housed Karl's office.

When she entered, she saw that the same man Karl had reprimanded on her last visit was sitting at the desk. He remembered her.

"Good day, Fräulein Hessler," he said. "You can go up; the colonel is expecting you." She was glad the man didn't mention the crowd outside, because she was struggling not to show her disgust.

Karl was standing by the window when she entered his office. She went over and stood beside him. The young woman she had seen cowering in the doorway was being pulled away by the SS, who were dragging her by her hair. Karl swore. It was one of the few times she'd heard him swear.

"The bastards," he said.

She didn't know whether he was cursing the Jews or the men arresting them, but then she remembered his protection of Schultz and his family's respect for women and liked to think he swore at the Gestapo and the SS.

He turned to her. "Forgive me, darling. How did you get through? The crowd are filling the square."

"I couldn't get transport so I walked here." "You did what?" he shouted angrily.

"I walked, Karl. It's not far."

"You must never do that again, Hildegard. If you cannot get transport, then please call me and I'll send a car for you. If you want to walk through the streets of Berlin, you can, but I will walk with you. The ruins of Berlin are no place for you to be walking alone."

"I'm sorry, Karl," she said in surprise.

"Please sit down there and wait for me," he said sternly.

She was hurt and had to conceal her anger at being treated like a child, but as he was fourteen years her senior, she realised that he probably thought of her as little more than that at times.

On the journey home, they drove much of the way in silence. When finally he pulled up in front of the house, she turned to face him.

"Are you still angry with me, Karl?" she asked.

He looked down at her, and his voice was gentle now.

"I am trying to be," he said, "but I am finding it very hard to be angry with you for long. You must promise me, though, that you will never walk around Berlin alone again. You are much too precious to me for me to allow you to walk about the streets or to become part of crowds like the one in the square today."

"I promise," she said.

She realised that Karl was growing ever more protective. Things were not the same anymore; there was change in the air.

Over the next few weeks, Karl's visits increased and frequent meetings were taking place at the house. She frequently and successfully carried out the process of photographing the documents locked in his desk. Then, towards the end of March, he said he would be staying for a few days this time. Hildegard sensed the tension building up over the war. Not only was the German army being pushed back on the Russian front with heavy losses, but she was also sure that an Allied landing was expected soon. No longer could she foresee the possibility of spending another summer at the house. She felt that every hour with Karl was precious and was pleased that they were to have a few days together when there would be no meetings.

As always, the time with Karl passed quickly. He said there would be a meeting on the fourth day. Hildegard prepared herself for the usual procedure afterwards but was becoming more and more reluctant to continue spying activities. She was feeling the strain more than ever now and couldn't see how she could go on for much longer.

When Karl joined her after the meeting had ended and everyone had left, he said there would only be a brief meeting the next morning; the rest of the day would be theirs. Therefore, before creeping down the stairs that night, she reminded herself that she could at least look forward to the following day.

The house was in darkness except for a light shining under the door as she approached the study. She opened it and found herself face-to-face with Schultz. Her eyes quickly scanned the room. Karl's briefcase was open on his desk.

"Schultz, will you please come with me?" she said after a brief silence. He hesitated before following her to the kitchen. They sat down at the table. Schultz was a man who never smiled. He was tall and thin and spoke with a voice that was flat, as though he was devoid of all feeling.

"Now, please tell me exactly what you were doing in the colonel's study. Don't tell me that you thought you heard an intruder, because we both know that's not true." His hands were shaking, and she realised that he was as nervous as she was.

"I was looking for information about a man who attended the meeting here yesterday. I want to know where he works and where he lives," he said.

"Why do you not simply ask the colonel?"

"I cannot do that, for the colonel might send me away.
I would be arrested."

"Are you Jewish, Schultz? Is that what this is about?"

"Yes."

"The colonel has given you sanctuary here; he protects you, doesn't he?"

"Yes, and I don't want to cause him any problems, Fräulein."

"Why are you trying to track this man down—and who is he?"

"He is a Nazi responsible for the death of my wife and children."

"I am very sorry, Schultz," Hildegard said, "but tell me, what do you intend to do when you find him?"

"I will kill him."

"Have you thought what might happen to the colonel if you did? He's been harbouring you here. He could be arrested too. Is that what you want to happen? Listen to me, Schultz. I don't think the war will continue for much longer. Perhaps no more than a year. The opposing forces may win, and, if they do, they are likely to track your man down for you. If they lose and we win, you can still track him down when the war is over. Surely it would be best to wait and see what happens."

"I have not been able to find out anything about him. I have only looked in the colonel's briefcase, and I found nothing there to help me. The colonel's desk is locked. Please don't tell him, Fräulein. I will do as you say. I will wait until the war has ended. If I am arrested by the Gestapo, they will kill me."

"My loyalty and my duty are to the colonel, Schultz. If he protects you, then I am sure he's right to do so. I have no wish to cause you harm, but you must keep your promise to stop what you are doing, for if it happens again, I shall not remain silent."

She went to the dresser and poured a tot of brandy, which she handed to him. "Take this with you back upstairs but first see that you leave the colonel's briefcase exactly as you found it and put out the light in the study."

She listened until she heard him go back upstairs and then went to the study to check that the light was out. Afterwards, she returned to the kitchen and sat there thinking about what had happened. *Poor Schultz, how terrible his life must be,* she thought. She would have liked to tell him she would help him, that she had a key to Karl's desk and they could look together for information about the man he sought. She felt helpless and sad—sad for Karl, for herself, and for Schultz.

This episode was enough to warn her off any further spying activities; she had done all she could under the circumstances. She now felt sure that Karl would want to return to active service if he didn't have to consider Elsa and herself. She resolved to try to convince him that they would be safe if he were to go. Karl was always at risk whilst in Berlin because the air raids continued and all major cities were being heavily bombed. He would be in danger if he went back on active service, but perhaps not at much greater risk than if he stayed in Berlin. She thought it might at least give both of them a chance of surviving the war. If he went, Herr Hucke would surely agree that there would no longer be any reason for her to remain in Germany. She would take Elsa to stay with Karl's aunt and escape back to England one way or another. Then, after the war was over, she could come back to confess her role in the war to Karl and seek his forgiveness. Maybe it would not work, any of it. But at least the idea gave her hope. If she were to tell Herr Hucke now that her usefulness here was at an end and just disappear, Karl would certainly go looking for her and would be led back to Lotta, which might well put the group in danger. She hoped, therefore, that she would be able to persuade Herr Hucke that it would be best for her to remain at the house while Karl was working in Berlin but at the same time discontinue her present spying activities, which were now too dangerous. She would give Herr Hucke the impression that there was a strong possibility of Karl returning to active service in the not-too-distant future. If he did not do so, they would have to review the situation, but she would definitely encourage him to go.

Hildegard finally went back to the bedroom and stood for some time watching Karl sleeping before lying down beside him. She remembered his words to her after their first night together, nearly two years earlier. He'd said the future might be only the next day or the next week, so they had to take what they could from life. She had never felt this more keenly than now.

The following day she remained in a pensive mood whilst waiting for Karl to join her. He came into the room smiling. "I am glad that's over," he said, referring to the meeting. "They have all gone now. Have you had lunch, Hildegard?"

"Not yet, Karl. I'll see what Frieda can offer us."

Fifteen minutes later, Frieda sent up omelettes and fruit.

"Would you like to go out for dinner tonight?" Karl enquired.

"That would be nice, but I feel a little tired, so only if we can spend a lazy afternoon together."

"Do you mean lazy as in bed?" he enquired with a grin.

She nodded. "Yes, something like that."

"My own darling little Hilda," he whispered as he put his arms around her.

"My own darling Karl, if I may call you mine," she said.

"Of course I'm yours," said Karl. "As soon as the war is over, we shall—"

She quickly put her fingers to his lips because she knew he was about to say they would be married. "Karl, my love, I belong to you but while we are at war, you are a warrior, and you belong to Germany. Remember that morning after our first night together in Berlin, when you said our future might be only the next day or the next week? Well, it is as true now as it was then."

He tilted her head and gently kissed her. "Two years ago I brought a frightened young girl here to live with me," he said, "but now I find I have a woman as wise as she is beautiful."

This was her opportunity to try to persuade him to return to active service.

"Karl," she said, "if you want to go back on active service, I want you to do so. I really can look after myself, you know, and Elsa too. I would take her to Aunt Christa if we were losing the war. An old woman and a child would be safe together, and I could escape into Switzerland. Don't think I want you to go, my love; I should be lost without you, my life would be empty, but I would feel even worse if I thought I'd prevented you from doing what you feel is right."

"Thank you, my darling," he said, "but for now I must continue with my work in Berlin."

She would not give up. She would raise it again in a few weeks' time. When Hildegard dined at the restaurant with him that evening, she was relieved that she'd made a decision to discontinue her spying activities, though she knew more problems had yet to be resolved. She sighed happily and suddenly looked up to find Karl studying her. He smiled at her and placed his hand over hers.

"Hilda," he said, "I want you to know that I have been happier in the last two years than I have ever been in my life."

"My darling Karl, they have been my happiest years of mine too."

"Then always remember that whatever happens in the future, nothing can take this time away from us. Nothing," he repeated.

"Yes," she said, wondering if she would console herself with that thought one day.

Karl visited again on two occasions within the next three or four weeks. During each visit, a meeting of senior servicemen was held, but on no occasion did she attempt any further spying activities. The day following his second visit they said goodbye as they had done so many times before, and Hildegard and Elsa stood waving as he drove off.

She still had not reported the episode with Schultz to Herr Hucke, and she decided that the time had arrived when she must do so. She'd planned to contact Lotta at the end of the week, but only two days had passed when she received a call from her early in the morning. Hildegard had just gone down to breakfast when Frieda said that her aunt was asking to speak to her. When she went to the phone, Lotta asked if she could come right away. She promised to leave immediately, right after breakfast, knowing that urgent information awaited her. Lotta had told her that she need only prepare for a short stay. She threw a few things into a small case and was soon ready to go.

Herr Becker drove her to the station. She was lucky to catch a train within minutes. This was the first time she'd been summoned so urgently. She wondered what could have happened. It might be, of course, that they'd received word back from British intelligence. She resolved, however, to stand firm on her decision to stop spying activities at Karl von Richter's house.

As soon as Hildegard arrived at the home of Herr Hucke and his wife, she could see that something was wrong. Lotta's suitcases were in the hall, and she looked ready to leave.

Herr Hucke immediately took her to his study. "Sit down, Fräulein," he said. He sounded worried. "I have sad news: the Gestapo have arrested Otto."

She looked at Herr Hucke aghast. "Oh no, not Otto," she said, shaking her head in disbelief.

"I am afraid so, but there is one thing we can be sure of, Fräulein. Otto will not betray us. He will never reveal our names to the Gestapo, no matter what they do to him."

"Poor Otto," she said sadly. "He was so dedicated to our cause."

Herr Hucke nodded. "Yes, he is a brave man. His arrest means that we must act quickly, before the Gestapo come for the rest of us. The net is closing in. German troops are being moved to France because they believe that a British and American landing will soon take place, but they don't know where. The French Resistance is carrying out many successful acts of sabotage against German troop trains and supplies, often because of information we have passed to them from the documents and maps you have photographed. We also know that Colonel von Richter has been given the job of eradicating the resistance groups and putting an end to the acts of sabotage."

She felt a sudden sense of guilt. What if Otto's arrest and almost certain death could have been prevented? Had she photographed the notes and records of the last two meetings, they might have contained something to warn of imminent arrests. The thought of that possibility would haunt her for the rest of her days.

Herr Hucke continued: "Our group here will be disbanded, so I am arranging for you to be met and escorted back to France."

She had no need now to tell Herr Hucke of her decision. Instead, she asked him how soon she would be leaving.

"Almost immediately," he replied, "but we must ask you to do one further thing for us. We need you to buy us time, time to dismantle the group and to get away before any more of us are arrested. It will not be easy for you, Hildegard, but it may be our only chance. Eva has already left the village, and Lotta will be leaving today to try to get to her sister in Switzerland."

Herr Hucke was looking at her steadily and studying her reactions as he spoke. "It is vital that our contacts in the French

Resistance are able to continue with their work. This could depend on you."

"Why on me, Herr Hucke? I don't understand. What can I do?"

"As I've said, you can buy us the time to reorganise and regroup.

We need a diversion. The only sure method of creating one is to remove von Richter from the scene. He must be killed, and you are in the ideal position to do it.

Hildegard had dreaded this day and known it might come, yet she couldn't accept the reality now that it had. She just stared at Herr Hucke in disbelief. "But we are lovers," she finally gasped in a small voice.

"That may be, Hildegard, but the affair between you will be over once he sees that you have betrayed him. Whatever you do, all will come to light. Even if von Richter were to survive, imagine what his position might be if the Gestapo see him as having housed a key traitor."

She was stunned. Herr Hucke's voice sounded unreal to her. She felt sick; her head was spinning as she sat staring at him, dazed and unable to speak. He continued talking but she had no idea what he was saying. Then she realised that he had taken a handgun from the drawer of his desk.

"I want to be sure that you know how to use this and to fit a silencer," he said, "so will you please do that now, Fräulein?"

She just did as he asked, automatically. Her hands were shaking, and her throat was dry. She still couldn't speak.

"Do you know if the colonel is in Berlin at the moment? He's not at his home, is he?" Herr Hucke repeated himself. "Do you know where he is, Fräulein?" He was shouting now.

"He's in Berlin," she said finally.

"Good. It's best that you do it there. Lotta will provide you with a suitable bag for the gun. I've booked a room for you at the Hotel Meisler for tonight. Tomorrow afternoon would be the best time, if that is possible. I am arranging for a man to be waiting for you in a car opposite the hotel beginning at four o'clock in the afternoon. He will remain there as long as necessary. He will take you into France and put you in touch with our contacts in Spain."

After that, Hildegard was conscious of Herr Hucke talking for some time, but she didn't hear what he was saying. It didn't really matter, she thought, because she wasn't going to do what he'd asked. There had to be another way, and she would find it.

Herr Hucke eased himself out of his chair, so she stood up, realising he must have finished. As they both moved towards the door, he put his hand on her shoulder.

"Do not let us down, Fräulein. Remember, there are many brave men and women both here and in France whose lives could depend on you. Do not let Otto's sacrifice be in vain."

These words seemed to bring her back to reality. Herr Hucke followed her out of the room as she went to join Lotta, who presented her with the bag in which she was to carry the gun.

"There is a train to Berlin early this afternoon," said Lotta. "Come and have lunch and then I will take you to the station."

Herr Hucke said that he had urgent work to do, but before he left, he came to speak to Hildegard once again.

"Your work here has been invaluable to the movement," he said. "You have served us well and have played a major part in what we have been able to achieve. Now it only remains for me to wish you goodbye and good luck with the rest of your assignment. I hope you will return home to England safely, Fräulein. We shall not forget you."

"Thank you," she said. Her voice was barely audible. "Goodbye, Herr Hucke, and good luck."

After they had eaten, Lotta busied herself with final packing. "I am leaving for Switzerland this evening," she said.

"What will Herr Hucke do?"

"He must remain here for the present," said Lotta. "He wants me to go to my sister because my work here is done now. He won't worry about my safety if I am with her."

Hildegard put the bag containing the gun and silencer into her own small suitcase, and when she looked up, she saw that Lotta was wiping her eyes. It was the first time that she'd seen her express any emotion.

Hildegard went over to her and hugged her. "Thank you for everything you've done for me, Lotta," she said. "I could not have done my job without you. Maybe one day when the war is over, we shall meet again."

"Yes, perhaps," said Lotta. They both knew it was unlikely.

As Lotta drove to the station, they said very little.

Each was lost in her own thoughts. When they arrived, Hildegard got out of the car with her suitcase and, smiling at Lotta, wished her goodbye.

"Goodbye, my dear," said Lotta, "and good luck."

As she drove off, Hildegard realised that she had never felt so alone in all her life. She wondered what she was going to do. How she managed to purchase a ticket for Berlin and get on the train, she would never know. She had caught a train for Berlin rather than for the station nearest to Karl's home because Herr Hucke had told her to go to the Hotel Meisler. She would decide what to do next when she was there. She could not have gone home feeling as she did. Once on the fast-moving train she sat staring out of the window at the rapidly disappearing ground below. It would be so easy, she thought, to just open the carriage door and jump out. Then she saw two fellow travellers watching her, perhaps guessing what she was thinking. She smiled at them and then straightened up in her seat. It was a foolish idea, she thought. Committing suicide would only bring unhappiness to Karl and would certainly not help fellow members of the Resistance, thus she ruled out suicide as a course of action. It would have been simpler anyway to take her cyanide tablets than to jump out of the train.

After that, Hildegard couldn't really concentrate on anything. Her mind raced as she struggled with conflicting thoughts. She decided to get to the hotel, and once alone in her room, she would have the rest of the night to think about what had happened.

When she arrived, they were expecting her. She ordered coffee and a sandwich to be sent up to her room and told the woman at the reception desk that she was tired and would be retiring early.

When at last alone, Hildegard splashed her face with cold water. Soon afterwards, the waiter brought her order. She didn't really want it, but after drinking the coffee she managed to eat half of the sandwich. Then she lay down on the bed for a few minutes but couldn't settle down, so she got up and paced around the room, still unable to think clearly. She went and stood by the window for a while, watching the people in the street below. At one point, she even considered phoning Karl and pretending that nothing had happened. She wanted to feel safe in his arms again. Finally, after exhaustion from pacing up and down, she lay on the bed and fell asleep. Two hours later, she awoke wondering where she was, believing she'd had a nightmare. But reality soon hit her hard.

She lay thinking about the two years she had spent with Karl, including the air raids on their first night together. The happiness they had shared, the love and protection he had given her, his gentleness, his attitude to members of his family and to Schultz... Then she remembered the rally in the square outside the building where his offices were located. How she'd felt then about Nazi Germany and decided to continue with her spying activities... She'd told herself at the time that she and Karl were casualties of war. Although she was convinced that he was not a Nazi, they were both soldiers and, sadly, fighting on opposite sides.

Later that night, she thought about Anna, Marcel, and Antoine as well as other members of the French Resistance and even those in the German Resistance movement whose lives Herr Hucke believed might depend on her future action. She remembered Otto, whose death she felt she might have caused because she'd failed to do her job. Perhaps she'd caused the deaths of others too, and it might now culminate in Karl's death. If only Schultz hadn't interrupted her that night, she might have continued with her job. Yet she knew that she couldn't blame him, for it was her own decision to stop all spying activities for good. The incident with Schultz had just brought things to a head. She would have come to the same decision soon even if it hadn't happened. Now Herr Hucke had asked her to buy them time. She may have failed Otto; she did not want to fail others.

In the early hours of the morning, she fell asleep once more, but this time it was more from mental exhaustion than physical fatigue. When she awoke, she was sweating and conscious of her heart beating loudly. She knew that she was in the grip of panic. Although she'd made no firm decision about what to do, she felt she was being pushed towards an inevitable conclusion—one that she did not want to face. It was the reason she was sent into Germany.

She bathed, dressed, and rang for coffee and food to be sent up to her room once more. As the morning progressed, she started to accept what she must do. *Poor Elsa,* she thought. It would be hard enough for her to face the loss of Hildegard's company, but whatever would it be like for her to lose her father, whom she adored? This made Hildegard hesitate once more, but something always seemed to come to her mind to balance her doubts. What of all the people on both sides who had lost fathers, sons, brothers, and sometimes entire families, as poor Schultz and many thousands of Jews had?

Once she'd made her decision, she began to act automatically; all her reasoning powers were finally exhausted. She would think about it no more. Her job now was to carry out orders. She settled her bill, trying to take comfort in doing normal things. She would go to Karl's quarters on foot, she decided. Even though she knew it was ridiculous, as Hildegard walked along the streets, she felt guilty at breaking her promise to him never again to walk there alone.

She was carrying her small suitcase as well as Lotta's bag which held the gun. As she approached the square, she put the suitcase in the doorway of a disused building on a side street before entering Karl's headquarters. The corporal who knew her was sitting at the desk inside. She presented her pass to him, and he informed Karl that she was there. Slowly she began to climb the stairs. Halfway up, she froze. She couldn't kill the man she loved more than anything in the world—it was physically impossible. Her legs wouldn't move. Tears were running down her cheeks. Then suddenly she imagined seeing Otto's tortured face twisted in pain. At the same time, she heard a movement from below, galvanising her into action again. She continued to climb the stairs. Could she do it? She stood for a moment and took a deep breath. Her hands were shaking as she took the gun from the bag before knocking and entering Karl's room. As she went in, he stood up and smiled.

"Captain Alice Grant of the British Army," she blurted as she brought the gun from behind her back and fired it.

There was a look of disbelief on his face as he slumped to the floor. She at once rushed over to him.

"Oh my God," she cried, "what have I done? This bloody war."

Kneeling beside him, she cradled his head in her lap. He was breathing heavily; she didn't know whether he was conscious or not. She kissed his forehead. "I shall love you until the end of my days," she said softly. "You were the love of my life. May God forgive me."

By now, he was struggling for breath. Taking his hand in hers, she gently squeezed it, and she thought he might have squeezed hers in return, but she could not be sure. He was trying to raise himself up when he gasped for breath and fell back. Karl von Richter was dead.

"My beloved enemy," she whispered as she gently lay his hand down by his side. "We didn't stand a chance, my love. We were their pawns; they used us both."

A few moments passed before she picked up the gun which she had placed on the floor and put it back into her bag. After closing the door behind her, she descended the stairs and reported to the corporal, who booked her out of the building. Then she retraced her steps, collected her suitcase that was still in the doorway, and walked briskly back to the Hotel Meisler.

Exactly as Herr Hucke had said, there was a man standing by a black car opposite the hotel. He was smoking a cigarette and wearing a cap, and in the dim light, she couldn't see his face. She waited outside the hotel for a few moments; then, as he was stubbing out the cigarette with his foot, she crossed the road.

"Hildegard Hessler?" he enquired, without looking up. "Yes," she replied, going to open the rear door of the car.

"No, get in beside me," said the man, speaking with a heavy French accent.

He took her suitcase and pushed it onto the back seat.

The moment she got in and closed the door, he drove off.

Driving very fast, he didn't speak again until they were outside the city. When they reached a remote spot, he stopped the car and pulled off his cap, throwing it in the back seat alongside her suitcase. Then he turned to her and spoke.

"I told you I would be bringing you out of Germany one day."

She looked at him in amazement and then realised who he was. "Oh, Marcel!" she gasped. "Thank God it's you!" They hugged each other. "Hold me. Please hold me, Marcel," she begged. "I have just killed a man. He was a good man and didn't deserve to die."

"Few of us do," said Marcel, and he held her close until she stopped shaking. "We must go now," he said gently. "I must get you to a place of safety."

"A safe house?"

"Not exactly... But it is the house of a man who is a sympathiser. He will not ask questions and will give us shelter for the night. Then we will leave early in the morning and make our way to a safe house where we can stay for a few days if necessary."

When they arrived at the man's house, they were taken to a small attic room. "We'll have to share this room," said Marcel. "You can have the bed; I don't mind the floor. I have slept in far worse places."

"Why don't we both just lie on the bed?" she said. "I think we are both mature enough for that, don't you? I shall be thankful just to rest."

They did as she suggested, dozing occasionally until first light, when they left.

"I think it will be best if you go back to being Nicole," said Marcel. "They could have been warned at the border control to look out for Hildegard Hessler."

"But what about my identity papers?"

He took a document from his wallet. "This should suffice for now. Where we are going is a little-used border crossing, and the guards there know me. I've deliberately led them to believe I'm a collaborator. Food is in short supply, and they are open to bribes, fortunately. I have one or two boxes of eggs in the car; I'll say they were left over from deliveries we've been making over here and offer to let the guards have them. There are many German sympathisers in France, you know. It is nothing unusual."

"And you fool them with your sheer audacity, Marcel.

Tell me—do you still own the farm?"

He was grinning. "I do, but I go there only to pick up supplies now. I have a manager who runs it for me. He is an old man, but he's been a farmer all his life and knows what he's doing."

"And Anna. Is she safe?"

"She left to join her husband in North Africa; the Resistance movement is active there. Your route home may well be via North Africa."

"How soon do you expect to reach the border?"

"We should be in France by early afternoon and reach a safe house by the evening. Do not worry—we shall make it."

"I owe so much to you, Marcel," she said. "I shall never forget what you have done for me. Never."

Everything went as Marcel had anticipated. They were thankful when they reached the next place and could eat and sleep. Once again, they shared a room, but each had a bed this time, and she was glad not to be alone. She had forced all thoughts of the last few days from her mind and tried hard not to think of Karl. If she did, she feared she might take the cyanide tablets that she still carried. So she was sure that having Marcel with her had once more saved her life.

The couple who ran the safe house were brother and sister and, like Anna, asked no questions. There were many brave and courageous people in France risking their own lives for people they didn't even know. Alice and Marcel stayed at the safe house for three days while Marcel arranged a meeting with a man who was able to make radio contact with a Spanish guide who would organise her journey back to England. On their last night at the house, Marcel explained that he would see her across the border into Spain, and there he would hand her over to the guide who was to escort her on the final part of her journey.

When the time came for them to part, she didn't want to see Marcel go, any more than she had when he left her to the care of Otto over two long years ago. As he kissed her goodbye, this time on the lips, Marcel whispered, "Get in touch after the war is over. Don't tell me your real name but remember that mine is Maurice Trenet. If you write to me at the farmhouse, I think it will reach me eventually."

Then he introduced her to Pablo, her Spanish guide, and told him to take good care of her because she was a very special woman. Within a day and a half, Alice arrived in North Africa by means of a small fishing vessel and was on a plane back to England.

Chapter 10

HOME AGAIN

It was raining steadily when the plane landed. Alice felt the rain on her face as she stepped down from the small plane and stood still for a few moments, breathing in the air. A man who was there to meet her introduced himself as Lieutenant Anderson.

"Welcome home, Captain Grant," he said. "You must be thankful to be back home in England again at last."

To be called Captain Grant seemed so unreal to her. All she could manage to say in reply was, "Yes, Lieutenant, I am indeed thankful to be home."

She was thinking to herself, I have no home here anymore. Home to her was a house on the outskirts of a small village in Germany, where she had lived for the last two years.

They took her off to a reception area at headquarters, where she was able to take a shower and have a meal. The next stage was debriefing, and in charge was Major Andrew Sinclair, the man who had interviewed her before she was sent away on the assignment. They could not know how much she had been dreading the time when they would want to coax out of her all the events of the past couple of years. Describing her journey through France and back, and the help she'd received from the brave people she'd met in the Resistance movements, both in France and in Germany, was easy, of course. British intelligence was aware of her activities at the home of Karl Von Richter and the information she had provided, but they were anxious to know about her final days in Germany, including the death of the colonel. With great difficulty, Alice related the final hours, but at no time did she reveal the extent of her relationship with him, telling them only the things she thought they might need to know. She had no idea whether they believed her story that she had been employed as a tutor to the colonel's daughter and had lived at his house in that capacity. It was not easy to explain her visits to German intelligence headquarters, but she concocted a tale that documents and packages for the colonel had sometimes been sent to his home, and as they were marked urgent, she had volunteered to take them to his offices in Berlin. She told them that in so doing, various officials at headquarters had got to know her by sight, which had helped her gain access to the colonel's office when she took his life.

The following day she was briefly interviewed again, this time by a woman, and afterwards she saw Major Sinclair once more. He told her that she was to have four weeks' leave, saying that he had arranged for her to spend the first two weeks at a pleasant place where army personnel were sent to recuperate. Describing it as a convalescent home without restrictions, he explained that she would be able to come and go as she pleased during the daytime and would receive any help and medical care that she needed.

She had to admit that it solved an initial problem for her; she preferred the thought of being amongst strangers for a while rather than having to make contact with anyone she'd known before she was sent away. All Alice wanted to do now was try to forget, to block out the last few weeks from her mind. Explanations and reminiscences were much too painful. Thus she was relieved to arrive at the home.

It was a beautiful place, set amidst rolling countryside. Although she tried hard to relax, she found it difficult. They had offered her counselling, but she had refused because she didn't want to talk to anyone about her private life. She had done her job and felt that they had taken enough from her. Her memories were her own, and she would cherish them for the rest of her life. She certainly didn't want to share them with strangers.

Towards the end of her first week, Alice was surprised to have a visit from Major Sinclair. He sat down with her in the large conservatory that overlooked the gardens. At first, conversation was stilted and amounted to pleasantries. He seemed to be hesitating, and she felt quite sorry for him because he was obviously not enjoying his job. After a while, he looked at her and smiled somewhat reassuringly.

"I have something to tell you," he said.

He knew it was not until the end of 1942 that British Intelligence had started to use women spies. Not many men or women had been sent into Germany at any time during the war but in Hildegard's case, it had been special because the request had come early in 1942 from the German Resistance itself.

Now he had to bring her news concerning her personal life, some of which might be a shock to her, but he also had what he thought would be good news.

He looked at Alice and smiled reassuringly. "I have something to tell you", he said.

He was not sure how to put it to her. The fact that she was an attractive, young woman somehow made him feel all the more guilty for sending her on the assignment in the first place.

"Captain Grant," he said, "I didn't say anything when we last met because I felt you needed more time to accustom yourself again to your surroundings, but now I am very pleased to be able to tell you that your husband Philip Grant is alive and in a prisoner of war camp in Germany."

Alice just looked at him blankly. "Good Lord!" she exclaimed.

"You must be overjoyed," said Andrew Sinclair, trying to make conversation in the hope of lessening the shock. Alice was silent for a few moments and took a deep breath before she spoke. "I am overjoyed for Philip and for his parents," she said calmly, "but I have believed him dead for over three years, Major, so it's not easy for me to accept news like this."

"Yes, of course," he said. "I understand. It must come as a shock. I first learned of it when your husband's parents wrote to your commanding officer, saying that Philip had sent letters to you through the Red Cross but had heard nothing from you in reply. For security reasons, we couldn't tell them where you were, so I informed them that you had been moved to another unit and that details of your present whereabouts had unfortunately been temporarily mislaid."

"I'll go and see them. Will it be in order for me to tell them now that I was sent abroad?" Alice asked.

"That would be unwise," said Major Sinclair. "I think that for the time being, we should stick to what we have told them and not reveal anything about your assignment or where you have been for the last two years."

Major Sinclair was looking even more concerned now, and she could see that he had something else to say. "Now I have some sad news to tell you," he said gently.

She cut him short. "If it's about my father, I am prepared for that."

He continued: "Your father died just over a year ago. Once again, while you were away, I had to explain to the trustees of your father's estate that you were unable to contact them and that the administration of the rest of the estate would have to be held in abeyance, possibly for the duration of the war. You may certainly contact them now so that your father's affairs can be settled, but once again I must ask you on no account to reveal any information about your assignment or the reason for your absence."

"My father was terminally ill when I left," Alice said, "so I knew that he was unlikely to be alive. Have no fear, sir—I shall not give any information about where I have been or the reason for my absence."

Major Sinclair smiled at her kindly and patted her arm. "If there is anything at all that I can do to help you, Alice, please do not hesitate to call upon me."

"You are very kind, Major," she said. "I'm grateful for your concern, but I shall be all right."

Before leaving the convalescent home, Major Sinclair went to see the doctor who was in charge. The doctor welcomed him: "Come in, Major. I take it you want to talk to me about Captain Grant, and I am glad to have the opportunity to speak to you."

He sat down at his desk and beckoned the major to be seated.

"I realise you cannot discuss her health problems," said Andrew Sinclair, "but I am a little concerned about her mental state. Although I am not at liberty to give you the details, I can tell you that she has worked under constant pressure during the last two or three years in circumstances which few could even tolerate in these troubled times."

"Well," said the doctor, "I can assure you that her general health is very good, but as to her mental condition, I'm not sure. She seems extraordinarily composed, too composed one might say. My impression is that she may be in denial for some reason. There is little I can do to help her because she has emphatically refused counselling. I think, Major, that we shall just have to let things take their course and see how she adjusts. Only time will tell."

Major Sinclair left wishing there were something he could do, but he could only warn Alice's commanding officer that she might take some time to settle into army life again.

After Andrew Sinclair had gone, Alice looked at the piece of paper he had given her with the information about where to write to contact Philip. She still couldn't believe that he was alive. All the time that she was in Germany, he must have been there in a prison camp. She didn't understand why there had been no news of him in the eighteen months after his capture and before she was sent abroad. One thing was certain, though: she would not be able to resume the marriage when he returned. She hoped that Philip would feel the same way.

After thinking about it carefully, Alice decided not to visit Philip's parents but to write to them. She couldn't face the questions they were bound to ask, but she would of course write to Philip and make her letters friendly without being affectionate. It was going to be hard—she knew that—because she still could not live as other people did. She must always pretend that things were other than as they were.

After a few days, Alice left the convalescent home and booked into a hotel in Winchester, having made an appointment to see her father's solicitors. The senior partner, Thomas Pemberton, who was one of the trustees, was so considerate. He talked to her in a low, hushed voice, as though she had just been bereaved. She couldn't tell him that she had known two and half years ago that her father was terminally ill. She didn't want to have to find explanations for not having contacted him.

Once more, she had to lie, telling the solicitor that her father had kept his illness from her.

"I believe Major Sinclair explained to you that for security reasons, I was for some time unable to contact my father. I was involved in highly secret work. I am telling you this in the strictest confidence."

"Yes, I understand that, Captain Grant. I shall not make any reference to this part of our conversation in my notes," he promised her.

Pemberton produced a suitcase containing her father's personal effects including some items of jewellery which belonged to her mother and left her in the room to sort through them. Alice picked out one or two photographs but left the rest.

"Can you dispose of these things for me?" she said.

"We can do that, but what would you like to happen to your mother's jewellery?" he enquired.

"Oh, just sell the major items and give the rest to charity," she said dismissively. "I should like the estate wound up as soon as possible".

Pemberton seemed a kind old man and she felt sure he must think her cold and uncaring.

"I'm satisfied with the way you've handled my father's estate," she told him, and he looked surprised.

She couldn't tell him that she felt resentful about being sent away to be a spy at the age of twenty-three, and how even her father had thought she should agree to it. Alice stood up to go.

He opened the door and shook her hand. "I wish we could have met under happier circumstances, Captain Grant," he said.

Alice just nodded, knowing there was nothing that she could say.

After the meeting, she was glad to be out in the air, thankful that the ordeal was over. There were two weeks left of her leave, but Alice didn't really know what to do with them. She would prefer now to be working than to have too much time to think about the last two years. The next morning, she decided to return to her base. Her commanding officer welcomed her back, and she was pleased to see that some of her old friends were still there, Janet in particular.

While Alice had been away, Janet had married a captain in the army. Sadly, a few months after Alice's return, tragedy struck once more. This time, it hit Janet, whose husband was killed while taking part in the Normandy landings. Their roles were reversed when Alice tried to comfort her just as Janet had done when she'd heard that Philip's plane had been shot down. It was a difficult time for both of them. Alice could never tell anyone about her own loss, for her man had been German. She thought often of Marcel's words when she had told him that she had killed a man who didn't deserve to die: "Few of us do," he had said.

And that is true whichever side one is on, she thought.

In less than a year after Alice's return to England, the war in Europe was finally over. Nazi Germany had been defeated. Soon most of Alice's friends were returning home to try to take up their lives from where they had left them. As she herself had no family and no home to go to, she rented a cottage on the outskirts of Oxford. As for her career, she decided to become an interpreter, as she had claimed to be when in Germany. It was as though life had turned full circle.

Chapter 11

RETURN TO GERMANY

It was early summer, just as it had been when Alice first went to Germany during the war. She had deliberately taken a flight which took her only halfway to the house where she had lived with Karl von Richter. She wanted to travel by train for the rest of the journey because it would take her through the places she had come to know so well. It was now nearly ten years since Alice was last here. It had taken all that time for her to find the courage to return. Now she was coming back to face the past. She was doing it for Andrew as well as for herself.

Having managed to get a window seat, she glanced around the carriage at the other passengers. Most of the people seemed to be travelling alone, except for two women sitting opposite her, so welcoming the thought that it was likely to be a quiet journey, she merely smiled at the two women before settling in her corner to gaze out of the window. As the train rushed through many small stations, she thought about the years that had passed since she was last in Germany.

After the war ended, she had rented the cottage on the outskirts of Oxford for a year or so before moving into her own apartment. At first, she wasn't sure whether she wanted to stay in England or make her home in Switzerland, a country which had remained neutral during the war. Her career as an interpreter was extremely successful, and after a while, she had felt able to settle down.

Her personal life had been less successful. She soon lost interest in any man she met because the love of her life had already come and gone. Then she'd met up with Andrew Sinclair again at an army reunion. She'd liked him a lot but hadn't wanted anything more than friendship from him. Their friendship therefore remained a casual one over the years that followed, so it took her by surprise when, one evening after they'd had dinner together, he asked her to marry him. She hadn't accepted, but it made her realise that she wouldn't want to lose him. Andrew was the one constant feature in her life. His friendship had come to mean much to her.

From then on, she began to think of him differently. They had started seeing each other whenever they could, and they eventually became lovers. Andrew would be retiring from the army in a year or so and had hopes of them making a new life together. He'd again asked her to marry him. Although she hadn't accepted, she'd promised to think about it. She would have liked things just to go on as they were. She knew it wasn't fair to expect him to wait indefinitely for her to make up her mind. That is why, after many sleepless nights tossing and turning, Alice felt the need to reach some sort of decision. She realised that she had to come back to Germany to try to close that chapter in her life before she could even consider the prospect of marriage.

She feared loneliness and didn't want to remain alone throughout her life. She loved Andrew but just didn't know whether she loved him enough. Most of her friends were married now and had families, including Janet. If Karl had lived, she supposed that they too would have had a family by now.

Karl von Richter still dominated her life. Alice wanted to let go, but she didn't know how, so she was hoping that this visit would somehow enable her to put the past in the past, where it belonged. Then perhaps she would be able to marry Andrew.

Her thoughts were interrupted as the train rushed through the station where she used to alight when on visits to Herr Hucke and his wife, Lotta. She wondered what had happened to them after she had returned to England. She couldn't bear the thought that they might have fallen into the hands of the Gestapo, as Otto had done. *Poor Otto,* she thought. She was still haunted by the feeling of guilt over his death and the fear that if she had done her job better, she possibly could have prevented it. His was a terrible end. He was the bravest of them all and represented the greatest justification for what she had done to Karl to try to save others from a similar fate. She had vowed that never again would she become involved in war in the way that she had been. She'd seen too much suffering on both sides. Those back home who fought alongside their own people didn't understand what it was like. All these thoughts ran through Alice's mind as she stared out of the window.

The train would soon arrive at the station where she must alight. She was glad that she'd contacted the tourist office, because they had told her about a hotel which had been built at the edge of the village and which was ideal for her visit. It seemed an unlikely place for a hotel, but the village was only a few kilometres inside the western boundary, so perhaps that was the reason it had been built there. She had booked three nights at the hotel and would be able to walk into the village quite easily.

Apart from seeing the house that had been her home, Alice wanted to see Elsa again, so she'd written to her, asking if she could pay her a visit. Elsa was living in Switzerland now, but Alice's letter had been forwarded to her, and Elsa had written a curt little note in reply, agreeing, obviously with great reluctance, to meet her at the house in two days.

When Alice left the station, she was pleased that she'd arranged with the hotel for a car to meet her because there didn't seem to be any taxis in evidence. The train had made good time and arrived earlier than expected. She only had to wait a few minutes before she spotted a car with the name of the hotel painted on its side.

It turned out to be a modern well-furnished hotel, and she was given a large pleasant room overlooking the garden. She booked her table for dinner and later that evening made her plans for the following two days. She would take a leisurely walk into the village tomorrow. It would be interesting to see what changes there had been since the last time she was there.

Having slept well, Alice awoke refreshed and after breakfast put on comfortable shoes and set off on her walk. As she looked at the houses and shops on the way, she could see that there had been many changes, and she wondered if the drapery shop and grocery store, which had been the usual reasons for her visits in the past, were still there. She also looked at some of the people she saw, thinking that perhaps someone might recognise her, but no one seemed to. A polite old man wished her good morning, but he surely only recognised her as a stranger.

The drapery shop was gone, and in its place was a shop selling fancy goods and souvenirs as well as picture postcards on a swivel stand outside. The grocery store had been extended into the shop next door. She couldn't remember for sure what the neighbouring shop used to sell but thought it might have been second-hand books.

When she went inside the grocery store, Alice saw that it was staffed by a middle-aged man and three young girls, and although they were still selling groceries, there were also delicatessen and patisserie counters. It seemed so strange to be back after all these years.

She wandered over to the patisserie counter and couldn't resist buying a slice of apple strudel, remembering how Frieda used to make it as a special treat for Elsa. When she came out of the shop, she wasn't sure what she was going to do with it, so she stood in a doorway and ate half before disposing of the rest in a rubbish bin nearby. Then she went back to the souvenir shop and was idly turning the stand on which the picture postcards were displayed when she noticed a picture of the village as it used to be during the war. Alice took the card into the shop and an assistant came forward, probably the owner, she thought.

"I lived at Colonel von Richter's house on the outskirts of the village during the war," Alice told her. "I remember when this was a drapery shop. I used to come in here quite often in those days."

"I didn't know it then," the owner said. "I bought the shop about five years ago."

"I was going to ask if you knew what became of the assistants who used to work at the drapery shop," said Alice.

The owner shook her head. "I am sorry, Fräulein, but the shop was empty when I bought it."

Alice would have liked to have met Eva again, but Eva must have fled from the village, perhaps even from Germany, after Otto was arrested. She might have managed to escape due to the confusion that must have been created by Karl's death. Alice hoped so anyway.

She sauntered around the village, and when she came across a small café, she stopped for a cup of coffee. After that, she strolled back to the hotel and sat in her room contemplating her visit to the house the next day. From Elsa's brief note agreeing to see her, it was clear that the meeting between them would be difficult. She did not expect forgiveness, of course. How could Elsa possibly forgive someone who had deprived her of the love of a father? Alice didn't know what the outcome of the meeting might be, but she wanted a chance to explain about her terrible dilemma. How she had been caught between duty to her country and her love for Karl. She especially wanted to satisfy herself that Elsa was happy once more. Elsa had loved her as a child, she knew that, and Alice would not like to find that the hurt she'd caused her had made her a hard and bitter young woman.

The next day, Alice booked a taxi to call for her at eleven o'clock. She had put on a sleeveless dress and after breakfast returned to her room to collect a jacket and pull on a pair of flat shoes. She was hoping that Elsa might allow her to walk down to the stream at the bottom of the garden—a place that held so many memories for her.

When she arrived at the house, remembering her first visit there with Karl, Alice stood looking around for a while before ringing the bell. The door was opened by a woman who asked her to wait in the hall, so she sat down in a large armchair and waited for the woman to return. About ten minutes later, she reappeared and led the way to the room which had been Karl's study. When Alice entered, she could see that very little had been changed. Elsa was sitting at the desk. She was an attractive young woman, and Alice's first thought was how proud Karl would have been of her. It was a moment before she spoke.

"Hello, Elsa."

Elsa looked at her but did not smile. "Why have you come here?" she said sharply.

Alice had rehearsed what she would say, and she chose her words carefully.

"Not in the hope that you will forgive me, because I know that you are unlikely to do that," she said, "but in the hope that I can make you understand that I did not want to do what I did. I loved your father very much, and I would have rather taken my own life than his."

"Then why didn't you?" Elsa interjected.

"I considered it," said Alice, "but it would have achieved nothing if I had, and in doing so, I might have further endangered the members of the German and French Resistance I was trying to protect. I bitterly regret what happened, Elsa. I know that it must have devastated your young life. Even though taking your father's life was an act of war, I have never been able to forgive myself.

When I came here, I was little more than your age now—a girl sent to do a woman's job. I was a captain in the British Women's Army, and they sent me to obtain information about German troop movements, something in which your father was involved in with his work in German intelligence."

Alice paused, but there was no reaction from Elsa, so she continued. "I certainly did not expect to fall in love, but I did—hopelessly in love. Your father and I had two wonderful years together. He became the love of my life. Then one day I was told by the leader of the Resistance movement who gave me my instructions that one of our group had been arrested by the Gestapo... and that I had to buy them time by killing your father. At first, I made up my mind that I would not carry out these instructions, but then I wrestled with my conscience later. If I did not carry out my orders, I would be a traitor to my country and put at risk the lives of my colleagues in the Resistance movement. If I did as he asked, I would hurt those I loved most and ruin my own life at the same time. That was my terrible dilemma. In the end, I decided that I had to do what he asked. Your father was a good man, a brave man, and he was loyal to his country—and in my circumstances, I believe he would have done the same."

Elsa finally spoke: "Yes, my father was a good man, a soldier and a hero. You came here, wormed your way into our lives, and made us love you, and to me that makes you the lowest of the low."

Alice wanted to reach out to her, beg for her forgiveness, and make her understand that she had never wanted to hurt any of them and had grown to love them, but she knew that was never going to be possible.

"I am afraid, Elsa" she said, "that war makes heroes of some of us and demons of others, usually depending on which side we are on. To you, I am a demon, and I understand that, but I hope that one day you may be able to view it differently."

"I shall never be able to forgive you if that is what you are hoping," said Elsa. Then she opened the drawer and threw something on the desk. "Here, I believe this is yours," she said. "You left it behind with the rest of your things when you fled. I don't want it."

Alice picked it up. It was the locket that Aunt Christa had given her, and when she opened it, she saw that Karl's picture and the picture of Elsa as a child were still inside.

"Thank you," she said, although she realised that Elsa had returned it not out of kindness but more out of bitterness and to mock her.

Elsa didn't reply. Instead, she stood up. "Now I would like you to leave," she said. "I never want to see you again, so please don't contact me."

"May I walk in the garden before I leave?" Alice enquired.

"If you wish," said Elsa coldly.

Alice moved towards the door. "Goodbye, Elsa," she said. "Believe me, I am sorry for everything. I wish you a good life, Elsa."

Once again, Elsa did not reply.

As Alice walked out into the garden, she was taken back in time. *It all could have happened yesterday,* she thought. She wandered slowly down the winding path towards the stream and could see ahead that the summer house and seat were still there. When she reached the seat, Alice was about to sit down when she noticed a stone that had been erected nearby, and she went over to look at it. It was a memorial to Karl. On it were engraved these words:

In memory of Colonel Karl von Richter,
a good man, brave warrior,
and loyal son of Germany
1905-1944

Seeing the stone took her by surprise and was a terrible shock. She returned to the seat, and soon the tears began to flow. All the tears that she had never been able to shed before came flooding, and then she was sobbing uncontrollably. She must have been there for at least half an hour when Alice felt a hand on her shoulder, and she turned round to find Frieda standing behind her.

"Come, Hildegard," she said, "this will not do." "Frieda," Alice exclaimed in a choking voice. "Come back to the house now," said Frieda.

"No, you don't understand," she sobbed. "It was I who took his life."

"Yes, I know that, and I also know how much you loved him. Come now... Come back to the house with me," she repeated.

"No, Frieda, I cannot. Elsa has asked me to leave. Could you call me a taxi, please, Frieda?"

"Elsa has gone," said Frieda. "She left to catch a train back to Switzerland, where she lives, so come back to the house, and when you are ready to leave, I will take you wherever you want to go. I have my own car now."

Frieda walked Alice back and then sat her down in the kitchen and made coffee.

"You are very kind, Frieda," said Alice when Frieda placed a cup of coffee on the table and sat down with her. "The stone... took me by surprise. So stark, the words so simple... It just hit me. Perhaps I was wrong to come here, but I felt I must."

"No, no, drink your coffee," said Frieda, "and when you feel better, you can tell me what happened between you and Elsa. When she told me you were coming, I suspected that something like this might happen."

Alice finished her coffee before she spoke. "I've been unable to move on with my life since it happened, Frieda, unable to mourn even. I had hoped that sufficient time had elapsed for me to be able to talk to Elsa about it. I know that she will never forgive me, but I thought that now that she is a young woman, she might be able to understand more about what happened. I suppose it was foolish of me."

"You never know," said Frieda, "she may feel differently one day. She is to be married soon, and as she grows older, she may learn that things are not always as straightforward as they appear to be." Frieda stood up. "I will make a fresh pot of coffee now," she said, "and then perhaps you will have something to eat with me. Sandwiches, perhaps?"

"I couldn't eat very much, but one small sandwich would be nice," said Alice, who had managed to regain her composure. Frieda brought coffee and the sandwiches and sat down again.

"How is Herr Becker?" Alice enquired.

"He passed away," said Frieda. "We lost our son Eric towards the end of the war. Hans became ill after that and never really recovered."

"Oh, Frieda, I am so very sorry, and now you are all alone."

"Yes, except for my sister, but I continue to live here, and I am not unhappy now."

"Forgive me for not asking before. It must have been a terrible time for you, losing both of them like that."

"It was a bad time for many of us, my dear, but I am resigned to it now."

"How do you manage to run the house?"

"We have new staff now, of course, and two of them are resident. There is a handyman here too; we also have a gardener, but he lives in the village. Sometimes my sister stays with me as well, so I'm not lonely."

"What happened to Schultz?" Alice enquired.

"After the colonel died, the Gestapo came and took him away, and we never heard any more about him."

"Poor Schultz," said Alice. "The colonel protected him because he was Jewish, didn't he?"

"You knew that?" said Frieda, surprised.

"Yes, I asked Schultz one day. He admitted it, and I guessed that Schultz was not his real name. I have never believed that the colonel was a Nazi and was pleased when I discovered that he was protecting Schultz."

"We knew that the camps existed," said Frieda, "but it was not until the war was over that we found out that many thousands, including women and children, had died there. It was such a dreadful time. Many thousands of people were killed by the bombs too, and Dresden was razed to the ground."

"Yes I know," said Alice. "So much hatred and so much suffering on both sides, and again, on both sides, good men like the colonel pay the price. And the suffering doesn't just end when the war is over, does it?"

"Life goes on, though," said Frieda. "You are a young woman still, and you have a life ahead of you. It is the future you must think about now."

"I want to move on with my life, but I cannot forgive myself for what I did, Frieda. I suppose I want someone else to forgive me, and then perhaps I can forgive myself.

I have tried to forget, but despite the years that have gone by, I still haven't come to terms with it."

The older woman put her hand on Alice's arm. "You must come back here again because I think it would help you," she said. "You cannot change what happened in the past, my dear, so you must learn to accept things as they are now."

Alice had found kindness and understanding where she didn't expect it. "You are very kind, Frieda" she said, "but Elsa would not want me to come back here again."

"Don't worry about that. She need not know," said Frieda. "You could stay with my sister. She lives in the village now. Then you could come here as my guest. Elsa doesn't own the house; the owners are the trustees of the colonel's estate."

Alice smiled. "You were always very persuasive."

Frieda took Alice back to her hotel and said she would come to see her the next day, so when she heard someone tapping on the door of her room after breakfast the following morning, Alice guessed it was Frieda. A red-eyed Alice opened the door.

"I thought as much," said Frieda, pushing past her and coming into the room. "I can see that you have been fretting. Gather your things together. I am taking you to my sister. She's invited you to stay for a few days."

Alice was smiling now. Frieda was just as she used to be, she thought, looking after her and helping her as she had done when she lived with Karl at the house. In those days, she had probably thought of it as her duty to the colonel.

Soon her bags were packed and she was checking out of the hotel and on her way to meet Frieda's sister Erica.

In appearance, Erica turned out to be much like Frieda, although her dress was more conservative and she wore her hair in a huge knot. Erica insisted that Alice should stay for the week and made her welcome, but Frieda collected her early most days. Sometimes they would go straight to the house; other times, Frieda would drive her to places she'd been to with Karl and they would have lunch before going back. Then Frieda would prepare dinner while Alice sat in the garden. Although she no longer experienced the awful shock she'd had when she first walked down the garden to the stream, she still felt a pang whenever she saw the memorial stone. Most of the time, though, Alice was at ease, and many happy memories came flooding back about the time she spent at the house, memories of the years when she and Karl had been together.

At the end of the week, when Alice said goodbye to Frieda and Erica, she felt more ready to move on with her life than she had in the past ten years. She and Frieda had agreed to visit each other before the summer was over, and she was glad that she would be able to come back to the house without dreading the thought of it.

Now she was looking forward to going to the South of France, where she would at last be seeing Maurice, or Marcel, as she had known him when he was a member of the French Resistance during the war.

Chapter 12

REUNION IN FRANCE

It was nearly a year after the war had ended before Alice and Maurice were in contact again. After that, they kept in touch over the years. He was married now, with a family as well as a chain of successful restaurants which, she was soon to discover, had a reputation of excellence in the South of France. She was glad that at least one of her wartime friends had made a success of his life.

She couldn't wait to see him again and wondered if he'd changed much in appearance since she had seen him last. He'd saved her life when he brought her out of Germany, and it may be that she saved his indirectly. This could be a special day for both of them. Maurice had arranged to meet the train, and when it stopped at her station, a fellow passenger helped her out with her luggage. Before she had a chance to look along the platform, Maurice ran up to her, greeted her by her French wartime name of Nicole, and kissed her. They stood for some time with their arms around each other before he took a step back and looked at her approvingly.

"You are as pretty as ever," he said, grinning just as he used to do.

Apart from his hair, which had receded a little, she didn't think that Maurice looked much different. He collected her suitcases and led the way to his car. She smiled, somehow not surprised when it turned out to be a red sports car. He placed her cases in the boot and then hugged and kissed her once more before opening the door for her. They just kept smiling at each other, unable to contain their delight at being together again.

"I hope you have your identity papers with you this time," he joked.

The journey from the station was about ten miles, and they drove along winding roads before arriving at a villa located halfway up a hill, from which the view was breathtaking.

"Oh, what a lovely place, Maurice!" she exclaimed.

He was still smiling. "Come meet my family. I will bring your luggage in later."

A beautiful tall woman with long dark hair and tanned skin came out of the house. "This is my wife, Babette," he said proudly. Two young boys then ran out to join them.

"And these are our sons, Charles and Jacques."

Babette was obviously pregnant with a third child.

Alice couldn't help envying her. It was every woman's dream to have such a lovely family and home.

The villa was grand yet comfortable, with tasteful decorations and furnishings and there was a huge conservatory at the rear. In a way, it seemed almost too perfect.

An au pair, whom Babette must have chosen for her plainness, came and took the boys away for their bedtime drink, and when they had gone, a maid announced that dinner was ready. When the meal was over, they moved to the conservatory with their coffee and drinks, and Babette listened patiently while Alice and Maurice reminisced about their wartime years.

Maurice had met his wife six months after the end of the war, so she had known little about his activities when he was in the French Resistance movement, and it seemed to Alice that he had not revealed a great deal about those years. Babette certainly seemed surprised to learn that Alice had been a spy in Germany during the war, rather than in occupied France. Alice was worried because she thought that Babette might wonder why she and Maurice had formed such a close friendship when they'd known each other for only a short time, and she was concerned that she might not understand about the bond that is formed between people who have risked their lives together. She felt she had to explain.

"Maurice brought me out of Germany at a time when I would almost certainly have been arrested by the Gestapo," she told Babette. "I had killed a high-ranking German officer, and had we been caught by the Germans, they would have killed us both. It would not have been a quick death."

When she heard this, Babette looked interested. "Whatever was it like, living alone with the enemy for two years?" she asked.

Alice wanted to cry out, "Despite everything, they were the happiest two years of my life, until I was forced to do what I did," but she didn't. Instead, she replied, "Well, I had to be careful what I said at all times, and on occasions it was difficult not to show my true feelings."

The next day, Maurice announced that he would take her for a drive along the coastal roads to Marseille and then back into the mountains. Babette had asked to be excused from joining them because she was involved in something with the children, so Maurice and Alice set off to spend the day together. She wanted to talk to him about Germany and tell him about Karl and her relationship with him. When they left the restaurant after lunch in Marseilles, she told Maurice that she had things to say to him while they were alone together. Maurice drove to a quiet spot and stopped the car.

"Well, Alice, I'm curious," he said. "What is it you want to talk to me about?"

"I want to tell you about something that happened when I was in Germany, for I feel that I might be accepting your hospitality under false pretences, and I wouldn't like that. You see, when I was there, I did things that may not be acceptable to you."

"You won't shock me. We have all done things we are not proud of."

"Yes, that may be, but this is different. You may already know that I was sent to Germany because I was of the right description and background to do a specific job. My mother was German, you know, and German Resistance had a perfect cover for me in the identity of Hildegard Hessler. I was to get to know a certain colonel who worked in German intelligence and who was involved in troop movements, and then I was to report back whatever information I could obtain about his activities. British intelligence and the German Resistance planned every detail, but they hadn't counted on one thing. I was supposed to seduce the colonel, but it didn't end there; I fell hopelessly in love with him... and he with me."

She paused to see what effect her words were having, but Maurice remained silent.

"I was never a traitor, Maurice," she said. "I was torn between love and duty in the two years that followed, but I did everything that was required of me. I lived with him at his house and photographed secret plans and documents, then passed the films to my contacts. After two years, it all came to a head when Otto was arrested by the Gestapo.

You knew Otto, of course."

Maurice had not interrupted her, but when he saw that she was in tears, he put his arms around her. "My poor darling," he said. "None of us can help with whom we fall in love, even though we may know that it could lead to disaster."

"It was dreadful, Maurice. You have no idea. I was ordered to kill him to buy time for the French Resistance, who were committing acts of sabotage against German trains carrying troops and weapons. The colonel was engaged in tracking down the saboteurs, and when Otto was arrested, it looked as though they were on to some of us in the German Resistance too. I didn't know what to do. I wrestled with my conscience for the next twenty-four hours and finally did what they asked."

She had begun to shake; Maurice stroked her hair as he tried to comfort her, and Alice buried her face in his jacket.

"I'm sorry, Maurice," she said, as she moved away,

"but I have never been able to forget him. He was the love of my life. He is the reason I cannot settle. Andrew keeps asking me to marry him, but the thought of settling into a normal married life scares me."

She looked up at him and guessed from the look in his eyes that he was feeling some guilt about the part that he had played in it all.

He kissed her forehead. "I understand how you feel, you know, and what you have told me doesn't make me think less of you—in fact, quite the opposite. Now I am going to tell you something about myself that I have not told anyone before. Like you, I cannot settle. I am—"

"But you have a wife and family," she interrupted.

"Yes, but it is not enough," he said. "I am restless.

I feel I have to live on the edge, to take risks as we did during the war. I know that I have everything a man could want—a beautiful wife, two lovely children and a third on the way, and a successful business—yet still I am not content. I feel driven to take risks." Maurice shook his head and sighed. "I don't know how to resolve it," he said.

"I suppose I could do something ridiculous, like climb Mount Everest or become a mercenary, but somehow I don't think Babette would agree to that, and I have no wish to kill people anyway. I had enough of that when I was one of those saboteurs you mentioned. Instead, I have a cabin in the mountains, and when I feel restless, I take a woman there for the weekend. I never take the same woman there twice, and I tell them it is only a romantic interlude. I make excuses to Babette, telling her I have to be away on business, perhaps negotiating for another restaurant. You would be surprised how inventive I can be."

Maurice was the one person Alice knew from the war years who had made a success of his life. She was surprised to hear him talking this way, not to mention disappointed, because his success had somehow given her courage and hope for her own future.

"But doesn't Babette suspect?" she asked.

"Maybe, but she knows I get restless. She knows I have a problem, so neither of us says anything because we love each other."

"The war continues to claim more victims even now,"

Alice said. "We have a similar problem in a way, I suppose.

I hope Babette doesn't imagine that there is something going on between us as well. Perhaps we shouldn't have come out here today without her."

"Then we would not have had the opportunity to talk like this to each other, and I think it's important for both of us that we have. You know that you're very special to me, Alice, and even more so now," he said with sincerity.

When they returned to the villa, Alice was conscious of Babette's feelings. She liked her and wanted to make a friend of her. To allay any suspicions Babette might have had about her, she decided to tell her about Andrew as soon as she had a suitable opportunity—or at least to tell her that she was considering marrying him. She was glad, therefore, that Babette took her on her next excursion.

They went to do some shopping in a nearby town, and with Babette's help, Alice bought presents for the children as well as some expensive perfume for Babette. It was, of course, the ideal time for her to talk to Babette about Andrew, so she told her that he had asked her to marry him, adding that he would be retiring from the army shortly and planned to open a bookshop in Edinburgh.

Babette was visibly relieved as she continued to talk about their plans for the future, and Alice knew that she had been right about Babette's suspicions.

As soon as the family was together, Alice presented the children with their presents, and Babette showed Maurice the perfume she had bought for her.

Maurice pretended to be jealous. "Don't I get anything?"

"Well, what would you like?" asked Alice.

"I think I may have found the right location for another restaurant," he said. "I'll take you to see it, and you can choose a name for it."

"Only if we can all go," said Alice tactfully.

"Yes, of course," Maurice said, smiling and trying not to show his disappointment, "although I don't think the boys will want to see it again."

In view of what Maurice had said about his inventiveness, Alice was glad that what he was saying now about finding a new restaurant appeared to be the truth. Babette had lost her initial reticence, and she was becoming friendlier each day, so she didn't want her to have unnecessary cause for suspicion.

By the end of her second week at the villa, the hot weather was becoming too much for Alice, particularly at night. One night she found it unbearable and was unable to sleep, so she got up and went to sit in the conservatory, having picked up a long silk shawl to throw over her nightgown should anyone come down. She must have been sitting there for some time when Maurice appeared.

She reached for the shawl.

"No need to cover up," he said, "I shan't attack you.

Not with Babette and the family upstairs anyway, although I might if we were alone," he said with his usual grin.

Maurice switched on a fan, and as they both sat there, she soon fell asleep. After a while, Maurice picked her up, carried her up the stairs, and laid her gently on her bed.

She was still asleep when she turned onto her side. Maurice smiled down at her and stood there for a few moments looking at her before creeping away quietly and closing the door behind him.

In the morning, Alice waited until she was alone with Maurice to ask him if she had fallen asleep down in the conservatory, because she couldn't remember going back to bed. Maurice laughed and told her how he had carried her up the stairs and put her on her bed. She wondered why he could not just have woken her, and it occurred to her that he was probably paying her more attention than he should.

Alice's visit finally ended. She had said goodbye to Babette and the children, and she set off for the airport with Maurice.

"It has been a wonderful holiday, and I cannot thank you enough for your kindness and understanding, Maurice," she told him.

He did not reply, but a minute or two later, he pulled over to the side of the road. "Extend your visit for a day or two and come to the cabin with me," he said.

It was a few moments before what he had suggested sank in. "For a romantic interlude, you mean?"

"I am sure you know that it would be more than that for us. You must know how I feel about you."

"Dear Maurice, you are very special to me, but romantic interludes would not solve my own problems."

"Then let us at least spend a day together," he said. "You could change your flight and go back tomorrow. I should like to take you to my friend Pierre's restaurant for lunch, and I am sure that he and his wife would be happy to put you up for the night, or if you prefer, we could book you into a hotel near the airport."

After all his kindness to her, Alice couldn't see how she could refuse, and besides, she thought she would like to have an extra day with Maurice on his own. She was concerned about Babette, though.

"Will not Babette be expecting you back?" she asked.

"I can phone her from Pierre's restaurant," he said.

"Pierre is a good friend; he was in the French Resistance movement too. We often worked together, and I know that he would like to meet anyone who was involved with the Resistance."

They arrived at Pierre's place just after midday, and Pierre and his wife, Rosanne, joined them for lunch.

Once Pierre learned that Alice had been a British spy in Germany, he insisted they be his guests for dinner and refused to take no for an answer. He would prepare something special in Alice's honour, he said, and both he and his wife insisted that she stay with them overnight.

They offered Maurice accommodation too and prevailed upon him to stay.

After lunch, Pierre and Rosanne had things to do so Maurice took Alice for a drive along the mountain roads.

When they came to a place which was renowned for a beautiful view, he asked if she would like to stop there for a while.

"That would be nice," she said, not wanting him to spend the whole afternoon driving. As they sat looking down at the valley below and she was marvelling at the beauty of it all, Maurice suddenly pulled her round and kissed her full on the lips. To her surprise, she clung to him for a while. Encouraged by her response, he kissed her again, but this time it was a longer and more passionate kiss. He looked at her tenderly. "Come to the cabin just for an hour or two. No one will know."

She had meant to say that she would not, but the words didn't come out. Instead, she said, "All right," simultaneously thinking, *What the hell am I doing?* Even though she knew she shouldn't, she still went with him because at last she felt passion and excitement instead of feeling dead inside. Neither spoke again until they reached the cabin, not wanting to break the spell.

Later, when they returned to Pierre's restaurant, Alice thought that she saw a knowing look pass between Pierre and his wife. She was worried that Pierre might have guessed where they had been, but then she decided that she must be mistaken and that her suspicion was unfounded and probably fuelled by guilt. After dinner, they spent the evening reminiscing about the war years and talking about their hopes for the future.

The next day when they stopped for coffee on the way to the airport, they didn't say much. Alice looked at her watch and then looked up at Maurice and smiled.

He grasped her hand. "I love you, Alice," he said.

She pulled her hand away from his grasp. "No, no, my dear. Yesterday should not have happened. It is Babette you love."

"Yes, I do love Babette, but I love you too. I have two loves. You are wrong if you think this is something that happened yesterday. I first fell in love with you when I took you to my farm to escape the attention of the German captain all those years ago." He took her hand again. "I've been thinking... If you came to live in France, I could buy one of those small villas up on the hill for you. I can afford it, and I think it might be the answer to both our problems. You would have the freedom you want, and I would have Babette and my family—and we would have each other."

"To live here as your mistress. Don't you think Babette might have something to say about that?"

He looked almost desperate. "I think she might welcome it. At least she would know where I was and whom I was with when I was not with her. It is not unusual here, you know."

"You know it cannot be..." she said.

He interrupted before she could say anything else.

"You're not going to tell me that you don't feel for me what I feel for you, are you?"

"No, Maurice, but it isn't that simple. Remember, I played with fire once before, and look where it got me.

You may think that Babette would just accept it, but that would only be because she loves you and wouldn't want to lose you. You love each other, and you would be risking everything, not only losing her but also your family and home and everything you've worked for. I could never allow you to do that for me. You mean a lot to me, you know that. Too much for me to let you risk ruining your life."

He was clearly downcast. "Well, remember that the offer remains open should you change your mind," he said.

When Alice's flight number was called at the airport, Maurice pressed something into her hand. "Perhaps this will help you keep track of time and remind you of me.

I don't want too much time to elapse before you come again, my darling."

They embraced, and he looked so desolate when she left him that she almost turned back. As she walked up the gangway, she thought that leaving him standing there must be the second hardest thing she'd had to do in all her life.

Twelve years on and she was still trying to get over the first time, so how could she have risked falling in love again and ruining yet more lives?

When Alice opened the little packet he'd given her, she found a small gold fob watch inside, and she pinned it to her jacket. It was a memento of a love that could not be, but she knew that a special bond would always exist between Maurice and herself. Now she had to think about going back home again. She doubted that she would ever be able to completely close the chapter of her life of which Karl had been a part, but she had at last faced up to what she had done and had been able to mourn. She felt sure now that no one would ever take Karl's place.

Andrew would be waiting for her, and he was offering marriage, a home, and a new life to share. He had always been there for her, and she was grateful for his patience and understanding. It was a quiet love that they would share, and she thought that perhaps it was that way for most people.

Chapter 13

VICTIMS OF WAR

Alice had risen early and was waiting for Janet before preparing breakfast. The night before, they had been talking into the early hours. She had been telling Janet about her time in Germany during the war and about her recent visit to try to come to terms with what had happened when she was there.

This day, however, they had planned to forget about their problems and go out for lunch and then perhaps to see a play. Tomorrow was another day. They would take up their lives from there.

Andrew stopped off in the village to buy a mammoth bunch of red roses. The weekend had arrived, and he was due to see Alice again at last. When he arrived at her apartment, he rang the bell, as he always did, and paused a while before letting himself in with his key. He put the bunch of flowers on the hall table as Alice ran out to greet him.

"It's seemed more like twelve months than one month," he said, bending to kiss her.

"It's good to see you, Andrew." She smiled up at him, "I have so much to tell you, but first let's have a drink. I'll get some glasses." She called from the kitchen, "I bought some champagne—will you open it, please? It's in the ice bucket on the side table."

He was elated. He felt that something positive must have happened because of her trip.

"I have also booked a table at the French restaurant in Oxford for dinner," she added when she returned with the glasses. Only a week or so ago, Alice had wondered if she would ever go to the little French restaurant with Andrew again.

"Good," he said, smiling at her.

She thought it would be easier to talk to him if they were in a public place. She planned to tell him the truth about Karl and how they had fallen in love. After all, it had happened many years ago, long before she and Andrew became lovers, so he should not feel hurt, but she wanted him to understand that she'd been traumatised by having to take Karl's life. She didn't want to hurt Andrew and would never reveal to him the extent of her feelings for Karl von Richter or let him know that she doubted that she could ever feel quite the same about any man again.

Nor did she, of course, intend to tell him that she'd had a brief affair with Maurice, any more than she had told Janet the whole truth about that, although she knew that Janet, being a woman and more intuitive, had probably guessed.

After they had eaten, he ordered coffee and brandy for both of them, and she told him about some of the things that had happened when she was with Karl. Finally she told him about her recent visit. She was able to tell him how she had at last been able to mourn, saying that she felt she could now put the past into the past, where it belonged.

"I hope this means that we can plan a life together now," Andrew said tentatively.

"I hope so too."

"Then I think we have something to celebrate, don't you?"

"Yes, Andrew, I think we have." She smiled. She knew that she loved him; it was just that she found it so hard to imagine herself married.

"I can get away for a couple of weeks next month," he said. "Will you come with me to Edinburgh to meet my mother? We could look around and perhaps decide upon an area where we would like to live when I retire next year. It's only eight months away now, you know."

"Well, I suppose it would do no harm to look around, but there's plenty of time isn't there? I'd love to meet your mother, though." Alice felt that she might not be showing sufficient enthusiasm. Andrew's father had died some years ago, and Jenny, his mother, had married a man named Charles Campbell. Both were in their seventies now.

Alice knew from the start that his mother didn't take to her, any more than apparently she had to Andrew's ex-wife. When she mentioned it to Andrew, he said that it was because his marriage had been such a disaster. It might take some time, but he was sure that his mother would like her when she got to know her. After a few more days, there was still little change in Jenny's attitude.

Alice had been unable to avoid overhearing a comment by Jenny. She was talking to Charles, asking him why a good-looking man like Andrew, who must meet plenty of women, could not have found a nice Scottish lass instead of a German. It was clear to Alice what his mother thought of her.

When she and Andrew had been there a week, he suggested that they go to see some estate agents in the city to get an idea of the cost of taking on a lease of suitable premises. They spent the next day looking at possible shops, and finally they saw a large double-fronted one. Andrew decided it would be ideal, and the rent was not unreasonable. She could see that he was excited at the prospect of renting this particular shop and was already planning the layout and alterations he would need.

"It will take some time to negotiate and complete a takeover of the lease," he said. "The present owner wants to have the benefit of the Christmas trade before he goes, so I think I should start negotiations right away, as we might lose it if we hesitate, don't you agree?"

She could hardly disagree that it was an ideal location, and as he seemed to have set his heart on it, she went along with the idea. On the following day, they went to look around various areas on the outskirts of the city where they might want to look for a house. Although they made no decision about that, things were moving much more quickly than she had expected.

When they returned to Oxfordshire, and after Andrew had gone, Alice tried to visualise what life might be like for her in Edinburgh. She just couldn't see herself as a housewife giving Andrew the support he deserved. In a few years' time, she feared that she might end up like Maurice, taking refuge in affairs. The more she thought about it, the more she realised that Andrew's mother was probably right. She would never make Andrew happy, because she couldn't live the sort of life he wanted. On the other hand, she didn't know what she would do without him. She would be lonely and miserable; he had been part of her life for so long. It would break her heart as well as his to have to tell him that she couldn't go through with it, but as the days went by, she was becoming surer than ever that facing the truth would be better for both of them in the end.

Having made up her mind, she dreaded the time when Andrew would come to visit again, when she would have to tell him that they must finally part. When it did happen, he begged her not to make any final decision, but Alice had to be strong. "We would just be delaying the pain of parting, and that would make it worse for both of us," she told him.

In early autumn, nearly three months after she and Andrew split up, Alice went to visit Frieda, and while she was at the house, she felt more able to put her life into perspective. She was certain now that she had done the right thing. As with Maurice, the war had made her restless, and it might be that she would never marry again.

One day when she was feeling particularly lonely, she made a sudden decision to contact her agent to ask if he could find her an assignment, preferably in the States, which would last a few months. He had said there was plenty of work available in New York at the United Nations. A day or two later, he phoned back to say that it was all arranged. So she went to the States to see where she would be working and agree to terms. She also needed to find herself a place to live. She would keep on the apartment at home, she thought, even if she needed to let it for a while.

The interview was successful, and she had sorted out temporary hotel accommodation. She was now returning home to make the necessary arrangements and say goodbye to her friends for a while. When Alice arrived at the airport in New York, she decided to grab a quick lunch rather than have a meal on the plane. The restaurant was fairly crowded, but she managed to find a free table. As she was reading a magazine while waiting for her food to be brought, a man asked if she would mind if he shared her table.

She looked up. "No, of course not," she said, and continued to read her magazine.

"I haven't a lot of time. My plane is due to leave in half an hour, but I am never too keen on the meals that are served on board," the man said with a grin.

He was obviously English. She smiled. "I quite agree." "Are you flying back to England?"

"Yes, I am," she said, "and my plane is due to leave in half an hour too."

She wasn't particularly keen to make conversation, but he seemed pleasant enough and clearly wanted to chat.

"I'm making a quick visit to see my mother and my son, and then I shall be back here again. Do you live over here or in England?"

"I live in England at the moment, but I shall be returning here soon to work at the UN."

"By the way, my name is Alan Westbrook."

"I'm Alice Grant," she said, beginning to take more notice of him. He was probably in his late thirties, she decided.

"Is your son at school in England?" she asked, to make conversation.

"Yes, he lives with my former wife. I don't get to see him very often, I'm afraid. I'm an overseas correspondent with a television channel here in the States. I travel around the world but have an apartment here which is my base. Whereabouts in New York will you be staying?" he enquired.

"Oh, I've yet to find somewhere to live over here, so I shall be staying at a hotel for a while."

"You're not married, I take it?"

"No, I'm not," she said, smiling. "But you were once?"

"Yes, once, a long time ago."

"Would you think it very presumptuous of me if I asked if I could see you when you return?"

She looked at him again. He seemed quite nice, and as she knew no one in the States, she thought she might as well agree. They travelled back on the same flight, and he managed to swap seats with a man sitting next to her.

Then, before the plane landed, he gave her his telephone number in New York and asked for her number in England, so that he could phone her before he went back to the States. Alice didn't expect to hear from him again after only a brief meeting at an airport and a chat on the flight back to relieve boredom, so when she returned home, she soon forgot about the incident.

There was a lot to do in the three weeks before she was due to start the job in New York. She would arrange to see Janet before she left. She even planned a quick visit to Frieda again. She never wanted to lose her ties with Frieda or the house where she had spent those years, those halcyon days, with Karl.

She felt that it was still too soon for her to speak to Andrew, but she would write to him. They had promised each other that they would remain friends, so she would explain what she was doing and write that she would be coming home eventually. She kept hoping that he had decided to take the lease on the shop in Edinburgh because it would mean that at least one of his dreams might come true. Although she felt that she had made the right decision, Alice still missed Andrew very much.

She had done most of the things that she'd planned and was due to return to the States in just over a week. Before starting the new assignment, she settled down to complete the work she had received from her agent before she had accepted the American project. There were occasions, though, when she had time to pause for reflection about her decision not to marry Andrew; sometimes doubts crept in, but they were never strong enough to make her change her mind.

As soon as her work was finished, Alice flew to Germany to spend the weekend there before leaving to start the new job. Whenever she stayed at the house with Frieda, she felt relaxed. It had an effect on her which she couldn't explain. She thought often of Karl's words all those years ago when she first went to live with him and he told her that whenever he returned there, he felt at peace. When she left, although she could not say that she was happy, she was not unhappy either; she too felt at ease, more than she had for some time.

Unfortunately, her earlier stay with Janet and Jon had not been so tranquil. She could see that Janet was struggling to keep her marriage together, and sadly, as she watched them, she foresaw a losing battle. She was sorry for them both. If only the end of hostilities had meant the end of unhappiness, but the war went on claiming its victims. How much worse it must have been for the vanquished, she thought, and for those on both sides who had been wounded, some of whom had lost limbs. Karl had paid the ultimate price at her own hands, so she did not expect to find happiness herself now. She deeply regretted that it had affected Andrew. Janet and Jon didn't deserve to be unhappy either, and she was sad that she could do nothing to help them, except be there for Janet if she needed her.

Soon she would be leaving for the States. The summer was over now, and the autumn days grew shorter. The leaves on the trees were turning various shades of yellow and red. She was admiring the colours as she stood in her sitting room gazing out of the window across the lawns and watching the leaves fall victim to the autumn winds. Then the ringing of the telephone abruptly disturbed the peace. She was surprised when it turned out to be Alan Westbrook. His voice was bright, and he greeted Alice as though she were an old friend.

"What flight have you booked?" he asked. "I'll see if I can book the same flight. Perhaps we'll be able to persuade someone to swap seats again," he added, without stopping to find out if she would welcome his company.

As it happened, she did, because it would prevent her from thinking too much about the job she was about to start and whether it was a good decision to go to the States and leave her friends behind.

When they arrived in New York, it was about eight o'clock at night, and Alan suggested they have a meal before going their respective ways. They had dinner together and agreed to meet again when he returned from South America, where he would be spending the next few weeks.

Alice's work at United Nations kept her extremely busy, which was just what she needed. It left her no time to think about her problems, past or present. Keeping busy and letting as much time as possible elapse before thinking about her future was the best thing that she could do. After a couple of weeks, she received a letter from Janet to say that things seemed to be coming to a head, and that she and Jon had discussed the possibility of a separation, initially for six months. When Alice read the letter, she decided to phone Janet that same evening. If Janet needed her support, it was the one thing that might cause her to return to England. She was relieved, therefore, when Janet told her that she and Jon had not made a decision yet, but that if they did separate, it would be amicable. In any event, they would leave it until after Christmas for the sake of the children. *It must be so much worse to have to break up a marriage when there are children involved,* Alice thought. At least she hadn't had that problem herself, so perhaps she was lucky after all.

The weeks had gone by so quickly; she had still made no real effort to find herself a more permanent place to stay and had even begun to wonder if it was worthwhile bothering. Then one evening she had a call from Alan Westbrook. He was back at least for a week, so they arranged to meet again for dinner. He took her to an Italian restaurant not far from his apartment.

"The food is more interesting here," he said. "I don't know about you, but I get tired of American steaks and burgers."

"I am very European," Alice confessed. "I love French, German, and Italian food."

"We'll try a French place next time, then, but I don't know where there is a German restaurant round here."

It was obvious that he took their friendship for granted, but Alice really didn't mind because she'd made no other friends.

"So," he said, "you haven't yet found yourself an apartment to rent. Why don't you move into my place? There's plenty of room, and I am away far more than I am there. I could do with a flatmate to look after the place when I'm away. It would be worth it to me, and I'd charge a very low rent, less than half of what you are paying at that hotel."

"It is tempting," she said, smiling. "Thank you, Alan. I think I'll take you up on your offer."

It seemed a sensible idea from which they would both benefit, so before the week was over, she had moved into Alan's apartment. The arrangement suited them, and they enjoyed each other's company whenever they were there together, which was not very often.

As Christmas approached, Alice decided to go home for the holiday and return at the start of the New Year. Andrew had written to say that he was free over the Christmas holiday and had asked if he could visit her when she returned. She agreed because she felt that sufficient time had now passed for them to be able to resume their friendship. Only this time it would be different—more as it used to be in the early years when they first knew each other. Alan was also going home and would be spending the time with his mother and son.

So once again, they travelled back together. Andrew was at the airport to meet her. Although he looked a little surprised when she introduced him to Alan, he suggested they all have lunch together. They had caught an early flight, and as usual, Alan had declined to eat on the plane.

After Alan had left them, Andrew commented, "He seems a nice chap."

"Yes, but although he is my flatmate, I don't know him all that well because he's away most of the time," she explained.

Alice saw the look on Andrew's face and could tell that he was still hurting. She was glad that they'd decided to book rooms at a hotel for Christmas rather than stay at her apartment.

"Didn't your mother want you home for Christmas?" Alice enquired.

"She did, but I made an excuse not to go," he said. "She had invited some woman who is a widow, a daughter of one of her friends. I think she is trying to pair me off. She means well, but I'm afraid I'm not interested."

Alice knew that she could get him back if she wanted to. It would end her loneliness and make him happy for a while at least, but all the problems for the future would remain. And anyway, he had apparently already signed the lease on the shop in Edinburgh. He could dispose of it again, of course, and she could tell him that if he took on a shop in Oxford, they could stay together but not get married. But she knew that none of these things would happen.

Andrew was curious about Alan Westbrook and asked her many questions. She hinted that she found Alan attractive, which wasn't true, although she liked him. She just thought it might make Andrew look for someone else himself.

They enjoyed the time they spent together, though, and she encouraged him to talk about the shop. He was so enthusiastic that she was sure he would make a success of it. He reminded her of Maurice in that way, only Andrew just wanted to settle down to a normal married life. Alice pictured him with a dog and tending his garden at the weekends. *He needs a wife who will be at home to look after him*, she thought.

Although she had enjoyed the Christmas break, she was not sorry when the time came to return to New York and take up her work again. Alan travelled back with her, and they told each other about some of their problems. Alan was so easy to talk to. He'd had problems in his marriage similar to the ones she might have had if she'd married Andrew. Apparently, his wife had been unable to tolerate his lifestyle. He didn't blame her, he said, but it was his job, and he was never going to become a nine-to-five employee.

Alan had spent a few weeks on an assignment in the Middle East, and she had seen him occasionally on the television, reporting on the situation out there. Whenever he was due to return, he gave her a few days' notice, not that she expected him to do so, because after all, it was his apartment. He was due back now, and since it was early March, it was still very cold. In fact, it had been snowing for most of the day, so Alice thought he might welcome a meal at home on his return. She spent a couple of hours preparing a coq au vin, as it could easily be reheated at whatever time he arrived. She had already bought some candlesticks and a couple of candles to put on the table. She knew by now that Alan would not have eaten on the plane if he could avoid doing so.

When he arrived cold and hungry, she was pleased that she had made the special effort to welcome him, and the meal was a great success. Afterwards, he told her about some of the things that had happened on his latest assignment.

They got on so well together that things just evolved from there. They had gone from being friends to flatmates. Then they became lovers. It just happened somehow. It was not a great romance, but the relationship worked for them. Neither of them wanted marriage. When Alice's contract ended, Alan persuaded her to take on another six-month assignment. When that ended, she did the same again.

Chapter 14

IN LIMBO

After several months of separation, Janet and Jon had parted, so it seemed sensible for Janet to stay at Alice's apartment with the children for the time being. There appeared to be nothing certain in the lives of any of them, except for Andrew, who had left the army and was installed in his shop in Edinburgh. According to his letters, he was much enjoying his new life. When Alice had been in the States just over a year, she received a letter from him saying that he was engaged to a woman who lived in Edinburgh. Her name was Sarah. They planned to marry in two months' time. Andrew hoped that she and Alan would attend their wedding. After giving it a lot of thought, Alice decided that she would attend. Alan seemed not to mind; in fact, he suggested they book a hotel and take a short holiday up in Scotland. Luckily, he was able to take the time.

They flew to Edinburgh two days before the wedding and booked into a hotel in the city centre. The following day, Andrew and Sarah met them. They all had lunch together. Alice liked Sarah; although quiet-natured, she was friendly. She didn't know Sarah's age but thought that she and Andrew were probably about the same age. Sarah was tall, slim, and neatly dressed. Andrew had said that she was a widow from the war years. Alice wondered if she was the widow that Andrew had been avoiding initially, the one who was the daughter of his mother's friend.

It was a quiet wedding. Most of the people attending were Sarah's friends, but Andrew's mother and stepfather were there. Andrew said that he had invited Janet, but apparently one of her boys was ill so she had not been able to come. It was disappointing. Alice had felt a pang or two during the ceremony and had seen Alan watching her.

The next day, however, Alan was as full of energy as usual. He gave her a hug and said, "Come on—let's paint the town!"

"Let's do that," she agreed. "Where shall we start?"

She was laughing. Alan was so good for her. They were good for each other, she thought. Neither made demands on the other. They just enjoyed each other's company and kept their relationship casual.

They visited art galleries and went to the theatre a couple of times, where they saw Brecht's *Mother Courage and Her Children* and a modern play by a new writer. They made love on their last night in Edinburgh, laughed a lot, and caught a flight to New York early the next day. Then Alan had several assignments in South America. By the time they were over, so was the summer.

Babette had invited Alice and Alan to stay at the villa for a couple of weeks. Alan promised to do his best to make time to go but was never sure where he might be sent at short notice, so he couldn't promise.

Whenever she was home in time, Alice would switch on the television and turn to the channel for which Alan was working. He was quite often featured in documentaries, reporting on conditions in the countries he was visiting. She knew that his work sometimes involved his taking risks.

Alan's wife had left him because she could no longer live with the uncertainty of never knowing for sure when and if he would return. Alice could understand how she felt, but she herself had lived in circumstances where her own life was always at risk. So she had come to accept it as a way of life. Alan was at least not living a life where he was permanently at risk of attack.

Unfortunately, when the time came for them to visit Maurice and Babette, Alan was unable to accompany her. Alice wasn't too happy about visiting them alone because she had not seen Maurice since their brief affair. She was aware of the temptation that might arise for both of them. Consequently, she phoned Babette to say that they couldn't come. But Babette insisted that she come alone. Alice felt that she couldn't refuse.

Alice was looking forward to the break, and she decided that she would also take the opportunity to visit Frieda. She booked a flight which was due to land in France around midday. Maurice was there to meet her.

"Babette and the au pair have taken the children to visit Babette's parents," he said. "Babette phoned me this morning to say that they won't be back until late tomorrow afternoon. She's asked that you forgive her for not being here to welcome you and says she's looking forward to seeing you tomorrow."

This was something that Alice had not expected and was the sort of situation she'd feared, but of course, it could not be helped.

She smiled at him. "I shall look forward to tomorrow, then, and also to seeing the little one. She must be two by now. What's her name?"

"She's adorable," he said. "She looks like Babette. We have named her Nicole."

Alice was a little surprised at the choice of name and wondered if Babette remembered that that was her wartime name when she arrived in occupied France. However, she didn't comment on the choice.

"We'll get your cases from the car," said Maurice, changing the subject. "I thought we might visit Pierre and his wife for lunch, if you agree. I phoned them in advance, and they are expecting us."

Alice was amused because he had not given her much choice. Nevertheless, she would like to visit Pierre and his wife again, even though it brought back memories of her previous visit two years ago. Maurice must have realised that would happen. The magic between them was still there, and it would be easy to yield to temptation. She was feeling now that she should not have come alone. But this time after they left Pierre's restaurant, they returned directly to the villa.

"The maid will be leaving early tomorrow to stay with her sister for a few days, so I have given her the rest of the day to herself," said Maurice. "Your room is all ready for you, though, so I'll take up your cases."

After unpacking, Alice went down to the conservatory, which looked beautiful; many plants were in full flower, and it was much pleasanter than on her last visit, when it had been so uncomfortably hot.

Maurice came to sit next to her, and he took hold of her hand. "Why didn't you marry Andrew?" he asked.

"I couldn't accept becoming a housewife. I am still restless, Maurice, and I didn't want to end up seeking distraction and excitement elsewhere."

"As I do, you mean."

"Yes, that is just what I mean."

"But now you have a new love."

"It is not a great romance, Maurice, although we are fond of each other. We accept each other's lifestyles, but neither of us wants marriage. We like it that way. We have our independence and want no commitment."

Maurice turned to face her. "Are you happy?"

"As far as I expect to be. Yes, I suppose I am happy."

Maurice held her face in his hands and kissed her tenderly. "You deserve so much more."

Alice edged away from him. She knew that she must not let her feelings overcome her judgement.

"Nothing has changed, you know," he said. "The offer I made to you two years ago is still open."

"I still cannot accept it, Maurice, and I never shall."

"I love you. I want you so much," he whispered.

"It's no good," she said. "It just cannot be. You have everything to lose by such an arrangement. I do not."

"All right," he said. "I have to accept what you say."

He was quiet for a while. Then he asked her about her job in New York. They talked late into the night, stopping only for a light supper. There was always so much they wanted to say to each other.

When Alice went down for breakfast in the morning, Maurice had just returned from taking the maid to the station. He was in a cheerful mood, teasing her and laughing and joking as he always did.

"What would you like to do today?" he asked. "I have spoken to Babette again. She will definitely not be back until late this afternoon. I shall meet her train. We could drive into Marseilles this morning or just stay here."

Alice was still tired after her journey, followed by the late night, so she chose to stay at the villa. They went into the sitting room, and Maurice switched on the radio. There was a dance band playing, and he danced her around the room, laughing, until she shouted to him to stop and flopped down on the settee.

"I will take you and Babette out for dinner tonight," he said, "so you and I can spend the day here together."

He went off somewhere, and she closed her eyes.

When she opened them, she found that Maurice had returned and was looking at her.

She smiled. "What are you doing?" she asked.

"Don't fight it, Alice," he said.

"What do you mean?"

"We love each other. You know I would never hurt Babette. There is no need for her to know how we feel about each other. You are not committed to anyone, and I am the way I am. We can have so little time together, so we should make the most of it."

The inevitable happened, of course. They ended up in bed. Afterwards, she fell asleep and awoke to find a note by her bed from Maurice, telling her that he had gone to meet Babette and the children. For now, Alice was relaxed and happy. She would grapple with Maurice's logic another time, she thought. She dressed leisurely and then went downstairs to await their arrival.

It was so quiet. Then she heard Maurice's car pull up outside the villa. The boys had heard it too. Obviously Maurice had told them that she was visiting because they came in excitedly calling her name. They were followed by a pretty little girl with dark brown hair and ringlets down to her shoulders. Babette came into the room, full of apologies for not being there to greet her when she arrived. It was good to see them all again. Alice's conscience pricked at her whenever she thought about her time alone with Maurice.

Just as on her previous visit, the time passed quickly. They all laughed and talked a lot, sometimes going out for meals, at other times driving to the mountains or down to the sea. She was pleased to have renewed her friendship with Babette and promised to return as soon as she could, bringing Alan with her next time. She was glad when Babette accompanied them to the airport when it was time to leave, for she didn't want any painful farewells with Maurice.

Alice's next visit was to Germany. From the airport, she had only a short train journey to the station where Frieda was to meet her. So many years had passed since she had lived at the house with Karl, yet she still felt that she was going home.

After exchanging news, she and Frieda walked to and from the village with the dogs and planned their next few days. Alice didn't want to stay at the house overnight, so she stayed in the village with Frieda's sister, Erica. Frieda collected her each day and brought her back to the house. Sometimes they drove to the nearest town for the day. At other times, she would spend time at the house and walk in the garden, wandering down to her favourite spot by the stream. After dinner, they always sat talking. Frieda asked many questions about her life in New York. The day before she was due to leave, when they were having coffee after dinner, on impulse Alice told Frieda about her affair with Maurice.

"I feel so disloyal—not to Alan but to Karl," she confessed.

"That is foolish," said Frieda. "The colonel's no longer with us, and I have said to you before that you must let go of the past."

"Even after all these years, I still find that hard, Frieda. I suppose I have only myself to blame."

"No," said Frieda, "you have the war to blame. Now, from what you are telling me, you're heading for heartbreak yet again. You should end it now, while you still can."

"That's a decision I have already made," said Alice. "I know it must be my responsibility to ensure that what happened while

I was there never happens again." Frieda was like a mother to her, and talking to her, Alice felt that she had reinforced her decision.

Alice returned to the States once more. She had always accepted that her work in New York would only be of a temporary nature and that she would go back to England eventually. When she arrived at Alan's apartment, she found a letter for her from Janet. It seemed she had been working on a large property near Swindon which had required a major refurbishment. At the end of the assignment, the owner gave a reception. There she was introduced to a writer and journalist named Gregory Martin. They were attracted to each other immediately.

Alice was so pleased to hear Janet's news that she phoned her that same evening. It was good to talk to her. She sounded extremely happy. She said that Gregory had met her two sons, and that it was amazing how well they all got on together. Only three months later, Janet phoned to say that she and the boys were moving in with Gregory. They planned to marry as soon as she obtained a divorce from Jon. There should be no problem, she said, because Jon was in agreement. She was sure it would be an amicable divorce.

Alan had been away for most of the time since Alice's visit to France and Germany but had written to say that he expected to take at least six weeks' leave at the end of the next month. He would phone her, as usual, as soon as he had a definite date and time. She always looked forward to seeing him. She and Alan were friends first and foremost. The other part of their relationship always seemed incidental.

As Janet was moving out of her apartment, Alice thought it might be nice if she and Alan could go back to England. Although it was not so long since she'd had a two-week break, Alice decided to tak a little more time off while Alan was free. She felt that her chief would not object. More and more, she was beginning to feel that she should soon return home and give up the job she had at the UN.

Alan came back to New York as planned and jumped at the idea of spending time in England. As well as staying with Alice at the apartment, he would be able to see his mother and son while Alice visited Janet. Neither of them had realised before how homesick they were. So they agreed to return to England permanently when Alan's assignments were completed. Naturally, they would live together at Alice's apartment. Alan was sure that he could find an opening with the British Broadcasting Corporation.

When she was back in the States, Alice found herself counting the weeks and days until their proposed return home for good after Alan's assignments finally came to an end. The time could not pass quickly enough for her.

Then one Friday afternoon, after she had finished her work early, she called at the local grocery store to pick up some supplies. When she had paid for them at the counter, the checkout girl said, as though pleased to be passing on news that might not yet be generally known,

"Terrible about the television news presenter, isn't it?"

Alice was taken aback. "What do you mean? Which reporter?"

"Oh, the English one, I can't remember his name. He was shot in an ambush and so was his photographer."

"Were they badly hurt?"

"I think so," said the girl.

Alice knew that there was another well-known British reporter working for the same channel as Alan. She told herself not to panic and hurried home as quickly as she could. As soon as she was back, she switched on the radio. There was a news report due within the next half hour. She felt stunned and realised that she was shivering, so she poured herself a small glass of brandy, just as she used to do sometimes in the days when she lived a life of uncertainty. Then she waited for the news bulletin.

The announcement was the first item on the news: "It is with great regret that we have to report the death of Alan Westbrook. He will be sadly missed by many. It happened while he . . ."

She heard no more. She switched off the radio and just sat there.

It must have been an hour or so later, as Alice was still trying to collect her thoughts, that the phone rang. It was Alan's boss. He explained that there had been a clash between army and rebel forces. Alan and two other men had been caught in crossfire between the two sides. Alan and one other man who worked for the television channel had both been killed instantly. The third man was seriously injured and in hospital. He promised to phone again when he had more information. She asked if Alan's mother had been notified, and he said that he hoped to contact her within the next hour.

Alice decided to wait until his mother had heard the news officially and then phone her later that evening. She must concentrate her mind on practical matters. She knew from past experience that it was probably the best way of getting through the next few days. She would have to vacate the apartment as soon as possible. There was no doubt that Alan's mother would want to come over and would have much to do winding up Alan's affairs in the States. Alice's own assignment was due to end soon. She felt sure that under the circumstances, they would release her right away. She would pack up her belongings the next day, advise the landlord of the apartment what had happened, and pay any outstanding bills she could find.

When later she tried to speak to Alan's mother, his ex-wife answered the phone and confirmed that his mother had been advised and was, of course, devastated. She went on to say that she'd be staying with her for a week or two and would accompany her to the States when she was fit to travel. Alice promised to visit later, when his mother was over the shock. She'd never met his mother but felt that she might be able to bring her some comfortby assuring her that Alan had been happy while they were together, especially during the last few months.

The first thing the next morning, Alice telephoned the man who organised her work schedule and arranged to see his chief, who, as she had hoped, released her from her contract. Later in the day, she returned to the apartment and booked a flight home in two days' time. She was in the midst of packing her belongings when the telephone rang. It was Andrew. "We've heard the sad news about Alan," he said. "We are so very sorry, Alice. What will you do now?"

"I'm leaving the States and coming home. I have already booked my flight to Heathrow. I'll be glad to be back in England."

"Good," he said. "Most of your friends are here, and those who are not can more easily come to England than to the States."

It was ironic, she thought, after she had put down the phone: she came out here to escape Andrew and to get over what had happened between them. Now he was the first to make contact, and it was good to hear his voice. She returned to the job of packing, and half an hour later, the phone rang once more. It was Andrew again.

"Give me your flight number and time of arrival," he said. "I intend to meet the plane. We want you to come here to stay with us for a week or two. Sarah is insisting."

Alice felt choked up. "I am very grateful, Andrew, but . . ."

He cut her short: "No buts, Alice."

"All right," she said, "and thank Sarah for me. See you soon."

The next day, she was ready to leave and finally sat down to write letters. First to Janet and Frieda and then to Babette and Maurice. When she had finished, she looked around the apartment. She felt sure that Alan had been happy with her and had lived the life he wanted to live. They had both taken each day as it came, with no great expectations for the future. She knew that his one regret would have been that he had not been able to spend enough time with his son.

There was nothing for her now in the States. The sooner she was home, the better. She had no special plans for her future, and after a while, she would probably contact her agent back home and try to pick up where she had left off. She knew that there would always be plenty of work for her, both as a translator of books and as an interpreter. This time, she would plan to work in Europe.

The following morning she got to the airport early and went to a restaurant for a quick snack before she was due to board the plane. Whenever she did this, she would always think of Alan and how they first met. She wiped away a tear but shed no further tears. She knew that Alan would not have wanted her to mourn but instead to celebrate his life and the short time they had spent together.

Andrew met the plane as promised. After taking most of her luggage to her apartment, they took a cab to the station and then travelled by train to Edinburgh, where Sarah met them. Sarah knew that she would need time to rest and wind down and so dissuaded Andrew from taking her to see the bookshop until she was ready to take an interest. Sarah was a real homemaker—Alice could see that. Her mission seemed to be to cook, clean, and look after Andrew.

As the days went by, Alice began to relax and soon wanted to visit the bookshop. When Andrew took her to see it, she was impressed; it was so well stocked and well laid out, and she could see that it was his dream come true. Like Maurice, he was keen to expand. His enthusiasm was infectious. They even went together to look at another shop he had in mind. Upon their return, Sarah greeted them with tea and freshly baked scones. She was planning something special for their evening meal and had invited Andrew's mother and Charles to join them. Alice wondered what his mother's attitude might be towards her now. She had never been sure whether his mother didn't like her or just hadn't thought she would make a suitable wife for Andrew.

The evening went well, with Sarah serving a delicious meal. Afterwards, they all went to the sitting room, and Jenny and Sarah discussed an article they had seen in a magazine, while Charles, like most men, was curious about Alice's role during the war and the time she spent in Germany as a spy. Even now, she was still reluctant to talk about it much. She would probably always feel it to be an intrusion on her privacy, but she answered his questions politely until Andrew came to her rescue.

Jenny was much nicer to her than she had been before, but there could never have been the same rapport between them as she had with Sarah. Alice knew now that she had made the right decision. Sarah was the right wife for Andrew. She was pleased to see him so happy. It had taken some years. Now most of her friends seemed to be sorting out their lives at last. However, Philip, her former husband, was the one not succeeding. He was into his third marriage, and from what Alice had heard, it was not running smoothly.

At home once more in her own apartment, Alice felt emptiness. There were several letters awaiting her return. She read them and placed them aside. There were invitations from

Janet, Maurice, and Frieda, but she was not sure that she wanted to accept any of them right now. She thought she ought to get used to living alone at the apartment again.

She wandered around from room to room, putting things back in familiar places. Her housekeeper had kept the apartment tidy. But things had been changed around in her absence. After a while, she went over to the bookshelves and idly pulled out one of the books that she'd inherited from her father. She sat down to read it, but couldn't get in to it somehow and put it back on the shelf. It made her think of her father. Alice always wondered why he had shown so little interest in her after her mother died. Even when they had last met and said goodbye, she felt sure that he realised that it was probably for the last time, yet he had shown little emotion. They had grown too far apart. She supposed her mother must have loved him, and he had seemed heartbroken when she died. Of late, however, Alice had begun to wonder if things really were as they had appeared to her through the eyes of a child. He may have been a man who couldn't give or show much love, she thought. She wished her mother had lived and they had got to know each other as women. She had fond memories of her mother, but they were a child's memories.

She was lost in her thoughts when the phone rang. She picked it up slowly, not really wanting to engage in conversation.

"Are you alone?" the female voice on the other end enquired. "I phoned as soon as I received your letter, and when there was no reply, I guessed you were away."

"Oh, Frieda, I'm glad it's you. I have been staying with Andrew and his wife."

"I'm sorry about the sad death of your friend," said Frieda. "Unless you are already working, I should like you to come home here for a while. You always find peace here."

It was true, and apart from her own home, it was the one place where she wanted to be. She would be able to think more clearly again when she was there. Alice noted that Frieda had referred to it as "home", and that of course was how she herself had long thought of it. It was her home in Germany.

"Thank you, Frieda," she said. "I should like that. I will come at the end of the week. I'll let you know when."

Frieda was always like a mother to her. Alice smiled to herself. No one else could get away with telling her what she must do. Frieda was a wise woman, though, and she respected her opinion. She would always be grateful for her advice, even if she sometimes didn't take it.

When Alice alighted from the train in Germany, she took a cab to Erica's house in the village. The next day, she walked from there to the house. Frieda herself answered the door.

"I thought I would save you the trouble of coming to pick me up," she said. "It's so good to be here, Frieda. This place is the one unchanging feature in my life. It seems to me no different from when I first saw it. It has a peace and tranquillity that I have found nowhere else."

"Come in, my dear. You are home now and can rest."

Frieda always welcomed her with tea or coffee. They would sit down together to talk and plan their day, and this occasion was no exception. In the following days, as it was too cold to sit in the garden, Alice spent a lot of time in the kitchen while Frieda was there preparing dinner or in the upstairs sitting room, where Frieda would join her later. Sometimes she wandered over to Karl's piano and lifted the lid to touch the keyboard. Her memories were so vivid that she could still feel his presence.

Chapter 15

RECONCILIATION

When Alice's agent offered her a six-month assignment in Geneva, she accepted it at once. Having spent much of her life moving around, she had begun to tire of working alone at home. She thought a spell in Switzerland would be ideal. Remembering that she had once considered making her home there after the war, Alice looked forward to it and even wondered if it might be possible to find Lotta's sister and to trace Lotta and Herr Hucke. Unfortunately, despite all her efforts, she was unsuccessful and had to abandon the search. But she still enjoyed the time she spent working in Switzerland.

After another brief spell at home, she took a six-week job in Berlin. At one time, she had thought that she would never want to see Berlin again, but a small flat was made available to her, and it meant that Frieda could visit and stay from time to time. Alice was happy in Frieda's company. Together they explored the city and enjoyed its many new buildings and shops.

One day, though, when she was alone, she found herself standing in the square outside the old building that had been

Karl's headquarters. It was under American occupation now, but she didn't want to go inside because the memories of what had happened there would still be too painful. Karl's death remained vividly in her mind. She had re-enacted those last hours so many times.

After the Berlin assignment, Alice returned to England to work from home again for a while. Six months elapsed, and she was surprised how quickly the time was passing. Although she kept in touch with friends, she was much too busy to visit anyone and still had two lengthy books for translation. She was much happier now about working at home, perhaps because her attitude towards life was changing. She felt that she might at last have found the inner peace that she craved.

A few more months went by, and she was still working from home when Frieda phoned one day and announced that she was paying her a visit. As it happened, it was a good time for Alice to take a short break, and it would be good to see Frieda again.

When she saw her, Frieda looked different somehow. She was putting on weight... or was it that she was looking older? Alice herself was nearly thirty-nine and realised that she would soon be the same age as Frieda was when they first met.

After a few days, it was obvious that Frieda had something on her mind. It seemed Frieda was studying her. Then one day Alice discovered what it was about.

"It is not good for you to be working here alone all the time," Frieda said. "When you didn't come to visit, I thought at first that you had at last stopped living in the past and were making a new life for yourself. But that is not what I'm seeing."

If she had not known Frieda so well, she would have been annoyed and hurt by this unwarranted attack upon her. "I have found contentment, Frieda. I don't feel alone; I am at peace."

"Well, I think you have put up bars and built a prison for yourself, living on memories and in a fantasy world of your own.

What you have is fear, not contentment. You are afraid to live because you have been hurt and are afraid of being hurt again. You have one life, Hildegard, and you should be grasping it and taking the opportunities it offers, not afraid to live or love again. You are building a mausoleum for yourself, shrinking away from life."

Alice was desperately trying to find the right words to defend herself against this onslaught. In her heart, she knew that it was true.

Frieda reached out and patted her on the arm. "Think about what I have said. I know I'm right."

"I know you mean well, Frieda," she replied. "Perhaps I will ask my agent if there is a short-term assignment away from home that he could offer me. I suppose it could do no harm to get away for a bit."

As it happened, after Frieda had gone back home, her agent phoned to ask what progress had been made on the translations she had in hand. So Alice took the opportunity to enquire about fresh work. Although he told her that he had nothing to offer her just then, he said he was expecting a request for an interpreter to go to Brussels. A three-week conference was to be held there shortly. If this job materialised, he would certainly recommend her. Three weeks would not be too long, she thought, so she decided that if she were offered the work, she would accept it.

She got the job in Brussels, and just before the conference was due to start, Alice was looking through the list of delegates and noticed that the German delegate was one "Walther von Richter". *What a coincidence*, she thought. She knew, of course, that there might be other von Richters in Germany apart from Karl's family. In any event, there were no von Richter men left in Karl's family—they had all died before or during the war—but out of curiosity, she watched for the German delegate to appear.

Walther von Richter was a big man, tall and broad-shouldered, with straight blond hair. She would put him at around forty years old, and she noted that he had a pleasant deep voice. It seemed he spoke English and French well, and he had no need of an interpreter's services.

The job in Brussels paid well, so Alice was pleased when, following the first assignment, she was given two further short assignments. After that, she went back home to finish translating the two books. Varying the work like this seemed to be working well for her. Frieda couldn't accuse her of hiding herself away any more.

Alice had settled back to working at the apartment again, and late one afternoon, her doorbell rang. She was not expecting anyone and couldn't believe it when she opened the door to find Maurice standing on the doorstep. She gasped in amazement.

"Maurice, what are you doing here?"

"I was at a company meeting in London, and when it finished, I took a chance and came over here to see you. Sorry I didn't phone you first," he said.

"You'd better come in and sit down. You look exhausted."

He followed her through to the sitting room and sat on the settee.

"I'm going to make you a cup of coffee. Stay where you are and I'll be back in a couple of minutes."

She had never seen him look so tired and ill, she thought. She returned with the coffee and sat down beside him. He was silent for a while before he spoke.

"It's not true that I have been to a meeting," he confessed. "I came over here especially to see you. I have left Babette; she asked me to go. I don't know what to do." "Just drink your coffee and sit quietly for a while, and then you can tell me what has happened."

Maurice looked drained of energy as he leaned forward with his head in his hands. "It's my fault," he said after a while. "I had an affair with a local woman. I had been seeing her regularly, and Babette found out. The woman doesn't mean anything to me. I told Babette that, but she wouldn't relent. She says that she cannot forgive me anymore. Naturally, I don't blame her."

Alice did not know what to say to him, for she'd known that something like this was bound to happen one day, but it would not help him to say so. Instead, she asked, "Have you phoned Babette to tell her you are over here?"

"No. She doesn't care where I go—she said so."

"I am sure that's not true, Maurice, and anyway, have you thought about the children? They won't understand and will want to know where you are. Would you promise to stop seeing this woman if Babette took you back?"

"Of course," he said. "I love Babette."

"I'm sure the two of you can sort it out together, Maurice."

He took her hand and held it. "I know I have been a fool," he muttered.

She wanted so much to comfort him. She could not bear to see him so distraught. With Maurice sitting close beside her, all her senses came alive again, all the feelings that had lain dormant for so long returning. But she knew she must send him back to Babette and his family. They could have found solace in each other's arms. Instead, they just held hands. Sometimes they talked. Sometimes they sat in silence, the love between them unexpressed. When at last, tired and exhausted, he fell asleep, Alice gently removed her hand from his and then brought a blanket from her room to cover him up.

The next morning, while Maurice was still asleep, she decided to phone Babette. She didn't want to give herself any time to have doubts about what she must do.

"I have always known he had other women," Babette confided. She was obviously in tears as she spoke. "But I knew that he loved me, and he adores the children, so I just accepted it as the way it had to be. Then when I found out that he had been seeing this woman regularly, it was too much." She paused. "I would not have minded so much if it had been you, Alice," she said, "because I have always known that he loves you."

Alice had to think quickly. "There is a strong bond between us, that I do not deny," she said, "but it is you that he loves, Babette. He has told me that this woman means nothing to him, and that if you would take him back, he would promise never to see her again. He is wretched without you and the family. He says you mean too much to him for him to allow anyone else to come between you. I'm sure he means that, Babette."

"If he would only promise not to behave as he does. I think he knows that I cannot just accept it anymore." There was silence for a moment. "Where is he now?" Babette enquired.

"Asleep on my settee in the sitting room," said Alice. "He arrived on my doorstep last night, tired and exhausted. If I drive him to the airport later in the day and let you know when he is due to arrive, will you meet him, Babette?"

"Yes," she said in a shaky voice. Alice guessed that she was wiping away the tears. "And will you let him come home so that you can sort it out together?"

There was a long pause, and then she heard a choking sob. "Yes, and tell him I love him."

The brief visit from Maurice had opened Alice's eyes. When he had gone, she had shed tears herself but was glad that she had held back long enough for him not to know. Frieda was right; she knew that now. She'd been living in her own prison, dulling all feeling, instead of seeking a new life for herself. She must make changes. First she had to finish her outstanding work. This time, however, it would be with a different attitude.

Alice wanted to keep the apartment because she would always regard it as her home. None of her friends really understood what it was like to have no family and no family home to which she could return… and no one at home to welcome her return. Her apartment was her haven, so she would definitely not give it up. She would just make a few alterations, new furniture, perhaps.

She settled on a new sofa and chairs and went into Oxford to visit the various furniture stores. She eventually chose a terracotta settee and a large matching armchair, as well as a smaller chair that would have to be re-covered to match. The assistant said it would be six weeks before it could all be delivered, but that didn't matter, Alice thought, because she would take a long break before seeking assignments in Europe.

Not long after these decisions, Frieda phoned again; she sounded excited and said she wanted her to come over. Once more, Frieda seemed to have chosen the right time. Alice gladly agreed and booked a week at the hotel where she always stayed. She arrived in Germany in the afternoon, and Frieda came to the hotel later to have dinner with her.

"Tomorrow you will come to the house. There will be someone there I want you to meet," she said.

Alice laughed. "I'm intrigued. Whoever is it?" "Max's younger brother."

"Max's younger brother!" said Alice incredulously. "Are you sure, Frieda? Why have I never heard of him? Neither Karl nor Max ever spoke of him while I was here."

Frieda ignored what she said and continued: "He's a politician. His name is Walther, and he's a cousin of the colonel. I had never heard of him either, but he told me that he went to live in Switzerland before the war when he was just eighteen, and from then on, the family disowned him. He is a good man, Hildegard. He wants very much to meet you. I have told him what happened and shown him your photograph."

"If you have told him what I did to Karl, I'm surprised that he would want to meet me. Besides, if you have shown him a photograph of me when I was with Karl, he is going to be very disappointed when he sees me."

Frieda would not accept excuses. "I have shown him a recent photograph too," she said.

"All right, Frieda, but please introduce me as Alice, not as Hildegard. Hildegard doesn't exist anymore. What was his profession before he went into politics, do you know?"

"I'm not sure," said Frieda, "but I believe he was a curator of a museum when he was in Switzerland. He's not married."

When she arrived at the house the next day, Alice didn't know how she was going to deal with the situation. Of course, it might be that this man's desire to meet her was simply out of curiosity because, as a member of the von Richter family, he wanted to see for himself what sort of woman took his cousin's life. Yet Frieda seemed to be behaving like a matchmaker.

Frieda had gone off to look for Walther while Alice stayed in the upstairs sitting room awaiting their return. Suddenly, the door opened and in walked a big blond man. He stood looking at her for a moment before he spoke.

"You must be Alice?" he said. He gave her a smile which lit up his face.

"And you are Walther," she said, smiling in return.

Alice recognised him at once as the German delegate at the conference in Brussels. He was tall like Karl but broader in build, and apart from his blond hair, he bore little resemblance to him and, surprisingly, even less to his brother, Max. In fact, his joking manner reminded her more of Maurice.

He came across the room to six next to her. "I have been looking forward to meeting you," he said. "I believe that you and I have something in particular in common. We are both outcasts of the von Richter family; that will surely give us much to talk about."

"I feel sure you are right," said Alice.

"Perhaps in our own way, we can help to reconcile those parts of the family which remain?"

She was amazed at his perfect English. He spoke with only a trace of a German accent. *His easy and affable manner must be an asset to him as a politician*, she thought.

At that moment, Frieda returned. She smiled at them.

"Well, now that you have met, I shall leave you together while I go to the kitchen to prepare our evening meal."

"She pushed you into this meeting, I think, didn't she?" Walther grinned.

"Well, put it like this: Frieda is not a lady one can easily refuse, but that doesn't mean that I'm not pleased to be here," said Alice, laughing.

"Good," he said, "because I have no wish to impose my company on you if you would rather I went away."

She could tell that his concern was genuine, but somehow this man unnerved her. Yet she wanted him to stay. She was intrigued by him and wanted to find out more.

"I should like us to get to know each other. If I seemed unwelcoming, it was because it has come as a surprise to me to find that Karl had another cousin, a cousin that no one had ever mentioned," she said apologetically.

"I am afraid the family disowned me many years ago.

If you're interested, I'll tell you all about it later."

She imagined that he must have suffered a lot of hurt; she could see it in his face when he spoke of his family.

Remembering her own hurt over her father's lack of love for her, Alice warmed to Walther from then on. The more time they spent together, the more she liked him.

Frieda had prepared a special dinner for which she joined them. Later she left them alone again. It gave them the opportunity to talk about their lives before the war. By the end of the evening, Alice was looking forward to spending the next day with Walther. He had suggested that he call for her at her hotel, and a little of the excitement she had felt when she had first met Karl as a young woman was beginning to creep over her.

She and Walther spent the following day together and in the evening had dinner at a restaurant in a nearby town before he returned her to her hotel. Over dinner, he had explained how he came to be rejected by his family. At the age of eighteen, he had told his father that he didn't agree with the way Germany was being run and didn't want to join the Wehrmacht, as his father wanted him to, because he couldn't fight to support the country's leaders. Walther had said he was going to leave Germany and wanted to go to university in Switzerland, but his father had refused to listen and told him that if he did that, he would no longer regard him as his son or as a member of the von Richter family. From that day on, neither his father nor his mother, nor any member of the von Richter family apart from Karl, had any contact with him again. Apparently, Karl had got word to him when his father died, and Walther had written to his mother, but she didn't reply to his letter. He explained that he'd been able to put himself through university because he received money from a trust fund set up by his grandfather. The trust money could not be taken away from him. During the war, he'd remained in Switzerland, and after he left university, he became the curator of a museum there.

When Walther had told her all this, he took Alice's hand and held it while he continued. "My family branded me a coward and a traitor, but I am not a coward, Alice. I am fully prepared to fight and die if necessary for the things I believe in, but I cannot fight for just a flag."

She was moved by what he had told her, and she felt that Walther was a special man. When he left her that night, he kissed her, and she returned his kiss. Apart from anything else, Walther was a man she respected. He was far from being a coward; she thought him a very brave man. She knew how difficult it must have been for him to make a stand against his father and then face life alone without his family.

During the following days, Alice told him a little about her life with Karl, of her own torment and dilemma during her last days in Germany as well as when she had made the decision to take Karl's life and how difficult it was for her to come to terms with it.

She remembered Walther's words: "You must learn to forgive yourself," he had told her. He had loved Karl too, he said. He was his hero when he was a boy, and if there was one thing of which he was certain, it was that Karl would have understood why she did what she did. Karl would have forgiven her, because if he'd found himself in her circumstances, he was sure that he would have done the same. "You did what you believed to be your duty to your colleagues and to your country," he told her. "You too were a soldier." That Walther himself could forgive her meant more to Alice than anything else, for Walther had loved Karl too.

He had to return to Brussels, but before he left, he asked whether she might like to stay on with Frieda for a few days, as he expected to be back at the end of the week. She didn't promise definitely but said that she would talk to Frieda and see if she could rearrange her schedule. In fact, she had nothing planned. She just felt that she needed time to think about the last few days. Frieda, of course, pressed her to stay, but Alice felt that she was being swept along too quickly on a course that others had planned for her. It reminded her too much of how she had met Karl. It wasn't that she didn't like Walther—quite the opposite—but she wished they had met accidentally, perhaps at a function, rather than Frieda having planned their meeting, as she obviously had. Her instinct was to make some excuse and run, and this is what she did, much to Frieda's disappointment.

Once back home, she began to have regrets and wished she had stayed on after all. Then after a day or so, she was convinced that she had made a dreadful mistake and was afraid that she might never hear from Walther again. By the end of the week Alice decided to phone Frieda and ask if he was there and then tell him how sorry she was that she had been unable to stay on at the house until his return.

That evening, she picked up the phone nervously and put in a call to Frieda. She was taken by surprise when Walther himself answered her call. He explained that Frieda had gone to visit her sister.

Alice wasn't going to pretend to be casual. "Well, it is you I wanted to speak to," she said. "I wanted you to know how sorry I am that I couldn't stay for your return."

He sounded pleased. "Well, don't worry," he said. "We will arrange something else." Her heart danced with joy, and she was surprised at the extent of her reaction.

"I've just had a thought," said Walther. "I will be in Paris in two weeks' time. I have to attend a meeting there, but I think I could manage a couple of extra days—that is, if you would like to meet me there."

Alice didn't hesitate. "I love Paris," she said. "I lived there for a year when I was studying at the Sorbonne. I should love to meet you in Paris."

Walther booked a room for her at his hotel, and when the day came for her to go, she could hardly contain her excitement. When she arrived at the hotel, there was a bunch of flowers in her room with a brief note attached: *Sorry, I can't leave early. See you at breakfast tomorrow.*

Two wonderful days followed. They sat in cafés and talked as they watched the people go by. Paris was always so colourful, so full of interest, so exciting. They had become relaxed in each other's company and just enjoyed the scene. In the evening, they sat on a seat on the banks of the Seine and watched the boats as they passed.

Walther told her that he would be very busy for the coming six weeks. After that, he planned a short holiday when they could meet up again. Alice couldn't wait for that time to come around. However, the weeks passed with no news from him, except a postcard telling her that he could make no definite plans just yet. She thought of phoning Frieda again to find out if she had any more news. Then she had a bright idea: she would go into Oxford and order the daily German newspapers to be sent to her in the hope that they might contain news of the conferences and meetings he was attending.

At first, she could find no mention of any conferences or meetings that were taking place. Then one morning the post was delivered earlier than usual, and she opened the newspaper to read it whilst eating breakfast. There, on an inside page, was a picture of Walther standing on the steps of a public building in Brussels with a tall well-dressed woman. They were looking at each and laughing. There was a caption below the photograph: *Has von Richter met his match in more ways than one?*

Alice felt stunned. She got up and walked around the apartment from room to room. In the end, she sat on her bed. *I'm being silly,* she thought. *Walther's a politician. He meets all sorts of people all the time, and because he's not married, the newspapers are bound to speculate and build on rumours in order to sell their papers.*

It was a week or so before Walther phoned to say that he still couldn't tell her when he would be able to get away, but then he went on to say how much he was looking forward to the time when he would see her again. Although Alice was pleased, she still wondered if he was just making an excuse to let her down lightly, but she knew her mind was playing tricks on her. Another von Richter had come into her life and had made a greater impact on her than she had thought possible. Perhaps she should visit Janet for a few days and try to take her mind off Walther. It was ridiculous to behave as she was doing. In the end, Alice decided to chase up the firm responsible for delivering the furniture she had ordered, and when they told her to expect delivery sometime in the following week, she couldn't very well go away.

After the delivery was made the next week, she drove into Oxford one day to buy new cushions and lamps, and she generally busied herself with domestic matters. That same evening, she was actually sitting by the telephone, intending to speak to Janet, when it rang. It was Walther to say that he would be leaving in two days, and he asked if she could book a room for him at a hotel in Oxford or nearby. He said that he would phone again the next evening to find out what arrangements she had made and if it was going to be convenient. Alice made sure that it was, and when he phoned, she planned to invite him to occupy the spare room in her apartment rather than a room in a hotel. Everything was going well for her at last, but she reminded herself not to appear too anxious. *It might frighten him away*, she thought.

Walther always managed to take her by surprise. She was expecting him to catch a train into Oxford and had checked the times of arrival of trains from London. Instead, he hired a car at the airport and arrived sooner than she had expected. As soon as he came through the front door, he hugged and kissed her.

Alice showed him his room and then went to make a cup of coffee, which she knew he would prefer to anything else. When she came into the sitting room, he was standing by the window, looking out across the lawns. Like Karl, he was a handsome man, and her heart leapt when she saw him standing there.

They spent the evening talking about their lives, both during the war and since. Walther told her about his work and ambitions: how he wanted to help build a strong Europe, a union of countries that would work together and prosper, where war between member states would not be possible and where people could move about freely from one country to another. She shared this ambition, having seen for herself the devastation that war brought upon both sides and the effects it had on those involved years after hostilities had ceased.

After breakfast the next day, they went for a stroll together, and when they returned, she made a light lunch because he wanted to take her out to dinner. When she took their drinks to the sitting room after lunch, Walther came up behind her.

"I don't have to sleep in your spare room again tonight, do I?" he whispered with a glint in his eye.

She turned round to face him, and standing on tiptoes, she kissed him. "I don't suppose you will have to sleep in that room ever again," she said, laughing. "Now, I think I had better book a table at the restaurant in Oxford before I do anything else."

"Then come back and put on your green dress," said Walther. "The one you wore when we first went out to dinner together. Don't wear the locket, though."

Alice laughed to herself. *He's being very mysterious*, she thought, *but perhaps he knows the locket contains a picture of Karl.*

Just before they were ready to leave and she was about to put on her velvet wrap, Walther once more came up behind her, and this time he placed something round her neck.

"I hope you like it," he said.

When she went over to the mirror, she couldn't believe her eyes. It was a gold necklace with a large emerald drop in the centre and two smaller emeralds on either side. It lay against her skin above the V-neck of her dress. She was speechless.

"I bought it in Amsterdam," he said "and they have agreed to take it back if you would prefer something else."

"Walther, it is the most beautiful necklace I have ever seen... but you shouldn't spend your money on me like this."

"I never found anyone I wanted to spend my money on before," he said, "so please do not deprive me of that pleasure now."

"I really don't know what to say that would be adequate. Thank you, Walther."

He looked so pleased as he bent to kiss her lightly on the forehead. She had accepted the necklace because she was in love again at last. This time, she felt no hesitation or doubt about her feelings.

Alice had booked dinner at Oxford's premier hotel, and when they were seated at their table, Walther ordered champagne. After they had eaten first and second courses, he reached across the table and took her hand in his.

"Now you can have the remaining half of your present," he said, placing a small box on the table before her.

She opened it to reveal an emerald ring that matched the necklace. He took it out of its box and pushed it onto the third finger of her left hand.

"It's an engagement ring," she said.

"So it is," said Walther, smiling, "but now I must be serious. I love you so much, Alice. I've known many women in my day, but I have never really loved anyone before. To fall in love like this is new to me. I've waited all my life for you, so I hope you will accept the ring to mark our engagement."

"Oh Walther, dear Walther, of course I will accept it. I think I fell in love with you soon after we met, although I didn't know it then."

"How about getting married six weeks from now?" he asked. "It would not take too long to organise, would it? I thought we might have a reception at the house in Germany. If you agree, we can phone Frieda tonight and start to make plans."

"I hope we're not rushing it too much, Walther," she said.

"I don't want to wait, do you? Have you doubts?" he asked.

"No doubts," she said. She had been thinking more of Walther when she'd queried whether they were rushing into marriage too quickly, but he had clearly made up his mind. For herself, Alice was sure this time. She knew that she would never want to marry any other man but Walther.

Later they laughed together when she told him how worried she had been when she saw his photograph in the German newspaper and read the comment about his possibly having met his match.

Naturally, Frieda was overjoyed to hear their news. She said that Elsa was staying at the house for the next few days and she would tell her before she left. Alice knew, though, that Elsa would not attend their wedding. Elsa would never forgive her, and she still didn't recognise Walther as a member of her family.

She didn't tell Walther, but at times, when she was alone, Alice began to wonder whether they might have a child. She was nearly forty now, and her mother had died in childbirth. It was something she would have to consider carefully before even discussing it with him. She would be the last hope for the von Richter family to have an heir to continue the line, but the baby might be a girl, she thought. She was convinced, however, that in any event, the name of Walther von Richter would live on and be recorded in the history of Europe.

Before Walther returned to Germany Alice wanted to take him to the little French restaurant in Oxford which she had frequented so often in the past, so they went there on the evening before he was due to go back. Sadly, the visit was marred by an unfortunate incident. Sitting at a table next to them was a party of three men and two women, and halfway through their meal, some sort of argument developed. One of the men began to shout at the woman sitting opposite to him, and when she got up to go, he slapped her face quite hard and was threatening to do so a second time.

Walther immediately jumped up and went over to the man. "If you want to hit someone, hit me," he said.

The man looked Walther up and down. "I've no quarrel with you," he replied.

"Well, you will have if you hit a woman in my presence again," said Walther.

"All right, all right," said the man, sitting back down. The party left about ten minutes later, and Alice was worried that the three men might lie in wait and attack Walther when he left the restaurant. Although Walther spoke good English, he spoke it with a slight German accent, and the men might have noticed it. There were still a lot of bad feelings towards all Germans. She thought this might incense them even more, but when she mentioned it to Walther, he just smiled, told her not to worry, and said that men who behave as that man had were usually cowards. As for recognising that he was German, there would be a lot of prejudice against his fellow citizens for a long time to come. He told her that they would have to accept that. But he could not let it prevent him from doing what he believed he should do. Alice knew that he was right. They would have to face these problems together. She was fortunate herself because she was unlikely to be recognised as English by strangers when she was in Germany, but she knew there might be problems for Walther in marrying a woman who was English.

They had wanted to avoid too much publicity, so a day or two before the reception at the house in Germany, Walther and Alice were married quietly at a registry office in Oxford, with just Janet and Gregory present. Then, when they returned to Germany, in order to protect her, Walther was anxious to conceal from the media Alice's wartime history and her role as a British spy, but they would never disguise the fact that she was the daughter of a British diplomat. They had agreed that they would work towards acceptance of the past on both sides and co-operation for the future.

It was a glorious spring afternoon on the day of the reception, and their guests were gathered on the lawn. Alice looked round with contentment. She was surrounded by friends in the beautiful garden of the house that had so many memories for her. She was there with her husband, the man for whom she felt her whole life and all of her experiences had been a preparation.

Walther was talking to Maurice. There they were, a German and a Frenchman who fifteen years before could have been bitter enemies, but now all that was in the past. Half of those present were Walther's German friends, and most of the others were English. *How strange it all seems, she thought, and how good it is to see them all together in friendship. Has the war really been worth so many lost lives on both sides? If only it would now lead to permanent peace here in Europe. If it did, then those who died would not have died in vain.* She felt she now had a purpose in life. She would work with Walther to achieve the sort of Europe they both wanted.

Janet had sauntered down the garden and come across Karl's memorial stone, at the foot of which lay a little bunch of forget-me-nots, now fading. She was reading the inscription when Andrew came and stood beside her.

"Well, she's a von Richter at last," he said. "That man has dogged my path and directed the course of my life from the grave."

"But you are happy now, aren't you, Andrew?" Janet asked.

"Yes, I suppose I am," he said, "but happiness is relative, isn't it?"

It was obvious that Andrew had never quite got over Alice, but perhaps that was poetic justice, Janet thought. After all, it was he who sent her to be a spy.

"And you, Janet, are you happy?" "Yes, I'm extremely happy," she said.

"Do you remember that day years ago when we met in Oxford by chance and unburdened our problems on each other over dinner?"

"I do, and it seems like a lifetime ago now."

"It didn't work out for either of us as we hoped it would at the time, did it? I suppose if I had known the outcome then, I might have played it differently," he said.

As they walked back to join the others, Janet linked her arm in his. "I think it has worked out for the best, though, Andrew," she said.

"My mother died last year, you know," said Andrew. "She never did take to Alice. She thought of her as German, and she hated all Germans until the day she died."

Janet sighed. "Nearly twenty years since it began, and the war is still affecting our lives."

Frieda had filled the house with flowers, and for the evening, Maurice had organised a lavish dinner. It had been a perfect day. Alice's only regret was that Elsa had not been present, but she knew that, sadly, there were those on both sides who would never forgive or forget. Elsa was one of them.

Some of the guests were staying at the house, but by the end of the following day, all had departed, including Alice and Walther, who had left for Maurice's small villa on the hill above his home in the South of France, where they were to spend the next two weeks. Only Frieda remained, with just her dogs for company. She looked out of the window across the lawn where the guests had gathered the day before and smiled. It was a smile of satisfaction; everything had turned out the way she had hoped. Whilst she was standing there, the two dogs padded into the room. First the big one came up to her and put his nose in her hand, and then the small one jumped onto the arm of the chair beside her.

"All right," she said. "We'll go into the garden."

It was already dusk as they went out onto the lawn and down the pathway. When Frieda reached the stream at the bottom of the garden, she saw the little bunch of now-dead flowers beneath the memorial stone, and it was not difficult for her to guess who had picked them in full bloom and placed them there. She stood thinking about the years that had passed since Alice and the colonel had lived at the house together. Then, after a while, Frieda voiced her thoughts to the night: "Rest in peace, Colonel," she said. "Your lady is family now, and I think she is happy again at last."

The End.

Milton Keynes UK
Ingram Content Group UK Ltd.
UKHW012007100124
435810UK00005B/216

9 781916 346406